in and down

a novel by
Brett Alexander Savory

BRINDLE
&GLASS

Library and Archives Canada Cataloguing in Publication
Savory, Brett Alexander, 1973–
In and down / Brett Alexander Savory.

ISBN 978-1-897142-26-4

I. Title.
PS8637.A88I5 2007   C813'.6   C2007-902549-8

Interior images: Homeros Gilani
Author photo: Glenn Grant

Brindle & Glass is pleased to thank the Canada Council for the
Arts and the Alberta Foundation for the Arts for their
contributions to our publishing program.

Brindle & Glass is committed to protecting the environment and to
the responsible use of natural resources. This book is printed on 100%
post-consumer recycled and ancient-forest-friendly paper. For more
information, please visit www.oldgrowthfree.com.

Brindle & Glass Publishing
www.brindleandglass.com

1 2 3 4 5 10 09 08 07

PRINTED AND BOUND IN CANADA

DEDICATION

"I am part of all I have met."
—Alfred Lord Tennyson

"Evil indeed is the man who has not one
woman to mourn him."
—Sir Arthur Conan Doyle

"What is our innocence,
what is our guilt? All are
naked, none is safe."
—Marianne Moore

PROLOGUE

TWO YOUNG BOYS—one eleven years old, the other twelve—walk on either side of their father, each holding one meaty hand. Lights blaze around them. Ferris wheels spin. Carnival barkers bark.

They do this every year, because every year the carnival comes to their town, and their father brings them here, doing his fatherly duty, spending time with his sons.

For one of the boys, the carnival is always the best thing to happen all year; the other boy is a little afraid of the carnival's presence. He wishes they wouldn't go so much. Sometimes he wishes they wouldn't go at all.

But a father will do what a father will do.

The first boy, the one who loves the carnival, he loves it because he feels it speaks to him in a way that nothing else in his life does. The clowns and other strange characters that dip and sway and carouse around him, he thinks he knows them well—he thinks he knows them from the inside. He comes to view the world through this yearly carnival, soaks up its desperation, its thoughtless glee.

This boy feels that the carnival somehow represents him.

The other boy simply puts one foot in front of the other, clenches his father's hand tightly, and hopes not to be swept away in all the madness. He has a fear deep down inside that he cannot name. A fear that he might get lost, separated from his family, and die here, forgotten by everyone, left to dry up and wither.

Blow away in the wind.

POOL

THE SUN SITS low on the horizon, but the water is still pretty warm—Stephen's treading it. Tiny, tiny bubbles surface as he paddles his legs. His arms do the same, but slower. Pushing out, pushing in. Staying afloat. His father reads a newspaper on the pool deck. Stephen's younger brother, Michael, smiles and cups his hands a few feet away from Stephen, squirting water as high as he can into the air.

The sun is hot on Stephen's face. It has been a few minutes now and his father has not looked up from his newspaper once.

Stephen turns to look at Michael. He watches his brother turn to look at their father. Their father doesn't look back, flips a giant double-page spread, snaps the paper tight, keeps reading.

Michael's squirting the water higher and higher, treading water himself. Getting bored with this, he sinks to the bottom and bobs up again, filling his cheeks with water so he can blow it out through a whale-like blowhole when he surfaces. Michael does this three times, but on the fourth trip down, Michael's head disappears beneath the surface of the water for longer than it should.

Stephen looks down into the water to see that Michael's got his legs caught in something. Thinking fast, Stephen dives down to where Michael struggles with whatever is wrapped around his legs. He locks eyes with his little brother, tries to convey the message: *You have to calm down and stop thrashing around, Mikey. I'll get you out of this.*

Stephen calmly unravels what he can now clearly see is a skipping rope. It drifts to the bottom of the pool while Stephen lifts Michael under the armpits, pulls him to the surface.

Both brothers pull in massive gulps of air. Their father is in the house calling 911. His face is not the face of a father who almost lost one of his sons in a drowning accident.

Stephen pulls Michael over to the ladder and, his lungs burning with the effort, hauls him out of the pool, lays him flat on the grass. Michael suddenly rolls onto his side, coughs up a gout of water. Stephen thumps his back, says, "That's right, get it all out, Mikey."

Stephen hears sirens getting closer, turning the corner at the end of the block. Car doors slam; booted feet slap the driveway. People dressed in white, carrying equipment, come around the side of the house.

Michael rolls onto his back and stares up at the darkening sky.

WEED KILLER

BRIGHT DAY. Really bright. In memory's eye, it's blinding.

Stephen is on the back porch of his aunt and uncle's place, fiddling with sticks. Michael has no idea what he's trying to do with them. It's just something Stephen does—fiddles about with sticks, sometimes moving them around in circles and semi-circles, clattering them off each other, as if trying to somehow communicate with them. The boys' father is out front, in the driveway with their uncle, fixing the car. The hood's up and the sun's glinting off it, making Michael squint whenever he looks their way from where he stands at the side of the house.

The house is big and white. Suburban, yet not in the suburbs. This is the country, but the house wants desperately to be from the outskirts of a big city.

Stephen shuffles his sticks around some more, repeatedly coming close to looking like he's actually doing something recognizable—if not trying to communicate, then perhaps playing a game of some sort—then the motions fall apart and he's back to simply fiddling again.

Michael looks back to the car and the sun has moved just enough for the hood to flash him straight in the eyes. He takes a step back, shielding his face and crunching gravel under his sneakers. Stephen looks up from his sticks at the sound. Then his eyes settle for a moment on a giant bottle of clear liquid to the right of the big wooden chair he's in. There is a hose attached to it, with a little black nozzle.

"Come 'ere for a sec, doofus."

Michael walks over to him. Stephen sets down the sticks. There is a matching wooden chair to the right of the giant bottle and Michael sits in it, rests his arms on the armrests.

Michael looks at him. "What?"

"Have some water, Mikey."

"Ya mean this stuff?" Michael points to the giant bottle.

"Yeah, it's really good. Fresh, you know? Good and cold."

"Alright." Michael leans over, grabs the hose. Brings the nozzle up to his mouth. Stephen goes back to fiddling with his sticks.

Michael pumps the nozzle a few times, aims it at his mouth. He swallows. Down it goes. Tastes a bit funny, but not so bad, really. He pumps some more in, keeps swallowing. Stephen keeps fiddling.

A few more squirts and swallows, then Michael hears Stephen chuckling.

"What's so funny?" Michael asks and sets the hose down.

"It's weed killer, doofus." Stephen turns to Michael. "I can't believe you just drank it. Couldn't you taste it?"

Inside Michael, alarm bells are ringing. *Weed killer. Poison.*

"Come on, Stephen," Michael says, heart beginning to pump hard, helping distribute the stuff through his system. "You're kidding, right?"

Stephen shakes his head, chuckling, and plays with his sticks some more. "Such a doofus," he says.

Michael turns to ice. His heart thuds harder in his chest. *I'm going to die now,* he thinks. He has never been so afraid in his life. "Stephen, it's not really weed killer, is it?" he whispers. He feels a vein trying to burst out of his head in the heat and silence of the day. Stephen says nothing. Michael imagines the vein popping and splooshing all over Stephen's sticks. Anger mounts, building in his skull, ferrying poison around his body. But he says nothing. He's not sure how he resists, how he calms himself, but instead of screaming at his brother he gets up from the wooden chair, walks slowly around the house and out to the front yard.

Michael's feet crunch more gravel, only this time it's really loud in his ears. He stops behind his father and uncle, who are hunched over his father's car, poking around under the hood.

"Dad?" Tentative.

His father doesn't hear him.

"Dad, we have to go somewhere," he says. His brain is making him say strange things. He's not being clear, but his father's not listening anyway.

"Dad?" Michael feels tears coming, but he doesn't want to cry. Not now. Even if it would get his father's attention.

"Dad, can—"

Michael's father looks over his shoulder and says, "Yes, okay, hang on; your uncle and I are talking."

His father and uncle are British. Some of their words sound strange to Michael's ears, like *hang* with its dropped *h*. He repeats this word to himself when he's alone. It tastes funny coming out of his mouth.

His father turns back to the car.

Michael tugs on his sleeve and says, "I swallowed weed killer." He could get to the point now. Now that his father had spoken, acknowledged his son, Michael could get to the point.

"You what?" his father says.

"Weed killer," Michael says, and points to the backyard. Now the tears are really threatening. They're glistening on his eyelids.

Understanding comes to his father; Michael sees it in his face. He sees that his father loves him. But at the same time, he also sees him cast a quick glance toward his brother. There is something in that look. Something Michael doesn't understand. Something that, perhaps, even his father doesn't understand.

Clock ticking. Every second that goes by, with every thump of Michael's heart, the poison spreads in him. He knows that Death, whatever that really means, is coming.

Suddenly, it is as though someone has pressed Fast Forward on the video machine of Michael's life and his father is picking him up in his arms and tossing him in the back seat of his uncle's car and his uncle is running to grab Stephen and they're on the road and going very fast and cars are whizzing by, whizzing by, going so fast Michael barely makes out their colours and then there are more colours because a cop has pulled them over for speeding and Michael's father explains what's happened, then they have an escort and they tear off the shoulder back into traffic and now—

Everything slows down.

Michael feels fine. Stephen is beside him, looking grumpy. He's playing with his sticks. Ever since Stephen saved Michael from drowning the year before, all he sees are those sticks. He fiddles and fiddles and barely looks up at Michael anymore.

Cars sail by in a hazy fog cloud. Michael sees all their detail. Colours are still flashing, but they're so slow they're like splashes of paint on the other cars instead of quick flashes of light. The colours drape themselves across the drivers' faces.

Stephen ignores Michael all the way to the hospital.

⚄ There are tiny bottles of medicine that make people puke. Michael is told to drink one of these. His feet are dangling over the side of one of those tables that has that thin, crinkly paper on it. Michael doesn't like these tables because of the paper and the sound it makes, so he tries his best not to move too much.

There is a large green bowl beside him.

Michael waits a few minutes, then a few more minutes, but still nothing happens.

"Do people usually throw up after one bottle?" he asks.

The doctor ignores him. His father and uncle watch him do nothing on the crinkly-paper table.

Stephen is out in the waiting room.

Another bottle is requested and he slugs it back, too. It tastes bad, but still nothing happens. The doctor and nurse are confused. Then the doctor finally answers Michael's question.

"Yes, son, one bottle should have done the trick. Half a bottle for most kids."

Michael nods, thinks about it for a second, then speaks. "So why hasn't it?"

The doctor gives him this look. "I don't know, son." The doctor drops his eyes, glues them back to his chart.

Two bottles later and the other staff have heard about The Boy With The Iron Stomach. Some of them peek in the doorway from time to time.

After the fourth bottle, Michael is still fine. The bowl next to him begins to look lonely and a little bit sad. He's almost forgotten about the weed killer and the threat of poisoning. So has everyone else. The event's focus has shifted to wondering how many bottles of puke-inducing medicine the freak boy can swallow.

Michael wonders if people are placing bets.

The fifth bottle arrives and Michael tips that one back, too. Nothing.

But then—

Quickly. Something. Shooting up his throat. He leans to his right, picking up the bowl to better his aim. He lets fly. When he's finally able to open his teary eyes, he sees the green goo slopping gently around inside. It is the same shade of green as the bowl.

"Feel better?" says the doctor.

A line of saliva is suspended from Michael's bottom lip, attached to the gloppy bile in the bowl. The doctor swims in and out of focus. "Better than what?" Michael asks.

"Well," the doctor says, looking confused again, "better than before."

"Before what?" Michael says.

The doctor glances at Michael's father, then his uncle.

Michael explains: "I didn't really feel all that sick in the first place, but I know I swallowed weed killer, and I know weed killer is poisonous, so I thought we should come to the hospital."

The doctor squints his eyes. "Yes, well . . ."

"Anybody ever swallow five bottles of that stuff before?" Michael asks.

"No," the doctor says. "Not that I've seen, anyway. You're the first."

"So I'm special."

Michael can tell that the doctor just wants to get out of here, but he needs to know if he's special. He needs to be told.

"I suppose you are," the doctor says. He clips his pen back into his top pocket, turns, and leaves the room.

"Special," Michael says to his back. "That's right. You suppose I am."

When Michael, his father, and his uncle get out to the waiting area, Michael approaches Stephen where he sits fiddling with his sticks.

"Stephen?"

"Yeah?" He still won't look at Michael.

"Please don't do something like that again, okay? I could have died, you know?"

Stephen says nothing.

Michael leans over and kisses him gently on the forehead. "Let's go."

On the way back to his uncle's house, Stephen doesn't play with his sticks.

GREEN SUIT AND TOP HAT

WHENEVER STEPHEN AND Michael stay at their uncle's place they sleep in bunk beds. Their cousins sleep in another set of bunks across the hall. Michael always gets the top. He likes the top, though, so that's fine. He thinks better up there.

Sleep comes easier up there, too. The window is left half open and night sounds creep across the ceiling and slither into Michael's ears. Crickets, wind rustling leaves, the occasional car whizzing by.

Stephen sleeps like death and Michael never hears him snoring. He barely even hears him breathing. Sometimes Michael climbs down the ladder, quiet as can be, to see if his brother's still alive. One time, he crept down and stared at Stephen's chest hard in the moonlight, waiting for it to rise or fall. After what felt like an hour, he had still noticed no movement. Michael panicked and started poking Stephen in the ribs. Stephen woke up slapping at Michael, asking him what in the hell he thought he was doing at two o'clock in the morning, poking him and waking him up. Michael just climbed up the ladder and tried to go back to sleep. He couldn't tell Stephen that he thought he was dead, that he was terrified of losing him. Because thoughts are powerful. Thoughts and ideas change people, change the world.

Beneath Michael, Stephen's breathing becomes measured, but his own eyes are wide open. It's time to think. Thoughts flit about in his head until he pays attention to them. Usually it doesn't matter so much what he thinks about just so long as he thinks about something.

Tonight, Michael thinks about the way his father looked at him today. He thinks about Stephen's indifference. He knows his brother loves him, but in a friend-like way, and he wants more than that. He wants him to be like a brother. The most important people in his life love him, but not how they should—or at least not how he wants them to.

Then he thinks about how selfish he is. He should be happy that he has a father and brother who care about him. A lot of kids don't have that. But still, he doesn't care that it's selfish. He likes to think that everyone is like this. Surely he can't be the only selfish one.

He would like to be able to tell them that he appreciates their love, but that they're going about it all wrong. He knows exactly how they should act and react in his presence. He feels that he could detail it all to them, then maybe they'd act accordingly.

Michael dreams a lot, and changing his family's love for him is what he dreams about the most.

Last night he dreamed about a man in a green suit and purple top hat. The man was smoking a very long cigarette and waggling his eyebrows at Michael. Big bushy black eyebrows. He was leaning on a cane, and he had very long fingers that draped over the knob of the cane and melted down its length.

"What are you doing in my dream?" Michael asked him very politely, as he'd been taught to talk to strangers.

"I'm not in your dream; you're in mine," the man answered, and waggled his eyebrows at Michael some more.

"How do you know?" Michael said.

"Because quite obviously I'm real and you're not. Just look at you."

Michael tried to bend his head down to look at himself but found that he could only move his eyes.

"I can't move my head, mister," Michael said. "Can you tell me what I look like, please?"

"Certainly. You're wearing a silly green suit and a very unattractive purple top hat. Positively ridiculous."

The man's skinny, dripping fingers shot back up to the rest of his hand like elastic bands. He winked at Michael and spun his cane.

"Well, that's exactly what you look like, mister. So how can you be so sure you're the one dreaming me?"

The man looked down at himself, moved the cigarette into a corner of his mouth, moved his hand to his hat and felt around a bit. "I say! Right you are, Mr. Head!" He brought his hand down to his cigarette, pulled smoke in, plucked the cigarette from his mouth, and blew white-grey rings at Michael. Before the rings reached his face, they'd turned into little waggling eyebrows.

"I wish," Michael said, "that I could move my head to see if you're telling the truth about my clothes. I don't own a green suit or a purple top hat. I'm only a kid."

"You can't move your head, but you can probably move your arms. Give it a try. Dreams have funny rules sometimes." The man tapped the knob of his cane twice with a drippy finger; only three of them slipped away from him this time.

Michael concentrated on moving his arms and, sure enough, up they came, up to the top of his head. He felt the smooth sides of the top hat. "So we're both wearing a green suit and purple top hat. Do you know where you got yours? I have no idea where mine could have come from."

Ignoring Michael, the man reached into his pants pocket and pulled out a watch on a chain. He puffed around the cigarette in his mouth. The cigarette, Michael noticed, never seemed to get any smaller. The man glanced at the face of the watch and gasped.

"Just *look* at the time!" he said. "I really ought to be going, Mr. Head." He crammed the watch back into his pocket.

"Why do you call me Mr. Head, mister? My name is Michael."

The man laughed suddenly, then quickly stopped. "Don't be foolish! You're Mr. Head. Now I really should be off, my boy. I'll be sure to—"

"Michael. My name's Michael."

The man puffed quietly on his cigarette, looking a bit put off that Michael had interrupted him.

"And you," Michael continued, "look just as silly as I must in that suit and hat." Michael didn't like it that the man wouldn't believe him about his name. And something about being called 'Mr. Head' upset him. It didn't sound like a real name.

"Well, there's no need to be rude," the man said, and motioned in the air at nothing. He waggled his eyebrows at Michael again, but this time without much spirit.

He tapped his foot and looked around, like he was waiting for a bus.

"So what are you waiting for, mister? Go on, then. Leave. Get out of my dream," Michael said, and waggled his eyebrows at the man.

The man didn't like that at all. With a loud "Harrumph!" he spun on his heel and walked quickly away from Michael.

Michael watched the man till he was very, very small, then he reached up to his head, pulled off the top hat, and held it out in front of him. Michael turned it toward himself and saw that there was something inside. He reached in and pulled it out.

It was a stick.

A thin, scraggly little tree branch with all the bark peeled from it, about the length of his forearm. He turned it over a few times in his hand, looked up into the distance at the spot where the man had disappeared. "What's this for?"

No answer.

Michael put the stick back into the top hat and placed it on his head again.

When he woke up, he told Stephen about the dream, and about the stick he found in the top hat. Stephen just squinted at Michael and said nothing.

"You think I should tell dad about it?" Michael asked very quietly.

"What for? It was just a dumb dream."

"Yeah, I guess. . . . What do you think it means?"

"I think it means you're a doofus." Stephen punched his brother in the arm, grabbed his sticks from his nightstand, and headed down for breakfast.

FLY

THEIR UNCLE'S HOUSE is always swarming with flies. No matter how much he sprays or how often he swats them, there never seem to be any fewer. Something about holes in the brick of the house. Even in winter there are a lot.

Sometimes Michael thinks his aunt didn't really die of cancer, but that his uncle has her stored somewhere in the basement or in the attic. He thinks that maybe his uncle likes the flies, and so he doesn't try very hard to kill them. They're a reminder of his wife, all carrying a piece of her around with them in their diseased bodies. Bits of auntie flying around the house.

To Michael, his cousins are like ghosts, flitting in and out of his peripheral vision; maybe they're playing downstairs, maybe outside, maybe on the moon. He doesn't care. And Stephen's with his sticks somewhere, maybe poking the bricks, checking for fly holes. More things that Michael doesn't care about.

After breakfast, their father's asleep on the couch, mouth wide open, a fly hangar awaiting an arrival. He's snoring and Michael's just standing over him, watching. Pity the fly without the strength to combat the windstorm in the hangar. He'll go down, sucked into the cavern, never to be seen again.

Here comes one—a tiny little guy. Buzzes around his father's head, spots the hangar, thinks about the warmth, maybe sizes up his chances against the storm. Smacks himself against a lampshade, rams into the living room window, crumples to the ledge, then zips away. Too small, anyway, and not so bright. Wouldn't have stood a chance.

Michael thinks that in the land of flies there must be legends about his father: The Storm That Few Have Weathered, they'd say—so many sucked into the gaping cavern; lost good men to that blustery boy, so we have; only the bravest of a generation try their luck. Only those without wives and children.

A fatter one dips in front of his father's face, testing the waters. Michael sees him zigzag in his path from the force of an exhalation. He's coming around again, though. A live one. He skims in close to his father's teeth, knocks against them softly, settles inside. The storm rages on, but Michael sees the fly brace himself against it, determined, his little feet glued to his father's tongue.

Michael wonders what Fat Fly is thinking. Is he disappointed with the experience? Did he think it would be more challenging? All the wild tales about the storm and now here he is, sitting in the middle of it, not even breaking a sweat. Hardly worth the fuss.

The fly walks around a little on his father's tongue. His father snorts, but Fat Fly doesn't flinch. Michael squats down and peers at the fly, up very close; the fly is unafraid. Michael likes to think that the fly's looking back at him, but with all those eyes, who knows what he's looking at?

Michael leans back and here comes another fly, maybe the first little one who'd originally lost his nerve. This one dive-bombs the first, but Fatty's not ready for the attack and they both go tumbling into the cavern. In and down.

Michael's father finally wakes up, coughing and spluttering. Michael doesn't tell him what happened; his father thinks he just got dust in his throat. It'll be Michael's and the flies' secret. Even though he doubts he'll ever talk to the flies about it, he's pretty sure they'll keep it under their hats.

Michael walks to the bottom of the stairs where he's about to find the letter that changes everything, and he suddenly realizes how wrong things must be for his father not to have asked Michael when he opened his eyes why he was just standing there, staring down at his sleeping body.

✿ The desk in the hallway at the bottom of the stairs has a drawer. The drawer is partially open. This drawer is never open. Michael has never seen it open, anyway. His feet carry him over to the drawer. He hears the strange-man-from-his-dream's voice coming from the wall beside the desk. He can't hear what the man's saying, but he thinks it's probably nothing important. Just more rubbish, like when he saw him last night—all funny clothes and subtle hints about nothing.

The envelope in the drawer is white, ripped along the top by rough hands. The letter inside is on lined yellow paper, one page. Now here come the words in the letter, all in purple ink. The letter is from Michael's mother, or so it says at the end. But his mother's been gone forever. There is no mother. There isn't any such thing as a mother.

It's dated three years, one month, and six days after Michael was born.

> I'm not coming home tonight.
> The boy makes me uneasy. You
> love him. I can't. You'll have to
> make dinner yourself. There is leftover
> shrimp in the fridge. Rice is next to the
> cupboard with the pots and pans. He
> doesn't feel like mine. I'm sorry.
> I'm not coming home tonight.
> I love you.

Words from Michael's non-existent mother. A strange emotion washes through him. He tries to cobble together in his mind a picture of his mother, what a mother should look like. He has never asked to see a photograph of her, and no one in his family does anything without being told.

Up the fourteen stairs, Michael hears Stephen clattering his sticks as he comes out of the bathroom and goes into their bunk-bedded room. Stephen shuts the door softly. The boys' father is still snoring in the next room, perhaps digesting bits of auntie through the bumbling flies in his belly.

The man in the green suit is whispering again in the walls next to Michael's head. The words are like the crinkle of hospital-room paper. Michael thinks that his uncle must have, until now, hidden this letter for his brother. Michael doesn't think Stephen would do something like that for him.

Michael knows the amount of steps in his uncle's staircase because Stephen once pushed him down them. He was six years old and just standing at the top, looking down, counting the steps over and again. He didn't hear Stephen come up behind him. Stephen shoved once, hard. Michael heard Stephen laughing at him all the way down. Michael bashed his face off the last step, twisted around as he came upright and cracked his skull on the far wall at the bottom.

The year after that, their father was ironing in the basement. Michael didn't know what an iron was, so he asked his brother. Stephen grinned and, when their father's back was turned, held out the iron, and told Michael to touch it. "Go ahead," he said. "It won't hurt, doofus." So Michael touched it. Not quickly, but as though it was just something to be held, like a toy. He wrapped his tiny hand around its edge. He screamed and cried. Stephen smiled and wandered away. Michael does not remember if their father reacted at all.

So he's pretty sure Stephen would never help him hide something, unless Stephen needed it hidden, too, of course. But then he wouldn't really be doing it for Michael, so that doesn't count.

Standing in the hallway, just thinking, letting his mind wander, Michael is finally able to make out some of the words coming from the wall, and he decides it's time to replace the contents of the envelope with a blank sheet of folded paper ripped from the notepad on the desk, next to the lamp. He stuffs the letter into his back pocket.

Time to talk to Stephen.

MOM

IT TAKES MICHAEL four tries to get up the staircase because he's counting them on the way up but keeps losing count because of the letter, and has to start again.

"Found a letter," Michael says when he finally reaches the top and enters his and his brother's room.

"Yeah, and?" Stephen says, flicks his eyes at Michael. He isn't playing with his sticks now; he has his nose in a comic book.

"From mom," Michael says, and waits for Stephen's reaction. Michael is always waiting for Stephen's reaction.

"Yeah, whatever." And Stephen's back to his comic book. "You're such a retard, Mikey. Leave me alone, would ya?"

"Look," Michael says, pulls the sheet out of his pocket, hands Stephen the letter.

Downstairs, Michael hears his father coughing and wheezing. He always coughs and wheezes when he wakes up from a nap. Michael hears the front door open, then his father and uncle are suddenly two big transport trucks taking turns rumbling low in their throats.

Stephen reads the letter. The comic book drops from his lap, forgotten. Spider-Man looks up at Michael from a two-page spread, ready for action.

"But we don't have a mom, Mikey."

"I know," Michael says, because he knows what his brother means. "But that's her name at the bottom. Dad told us her name, remember? That was it."

Stephen doesn't have to speak for Michael to know he remembers the name. Stephen's fingers shift to autopilot and start moving like they're playing with his sticks, even though his hands are empty. Fingers: twisting air, twisting paper.

"Here, you'll wreck it," Michael says and nips the sheet from his brother's hands. Stephen gets up, crosses the room to where his sticks are, grabs them, sits back down, starts fiddling. Wood on wood, shifting, tiny pieces falling off, drifting to the floor.

Michael feels like he has to try, even though he knows it's useless: "Stephen?"

Another flick of Stephen's eyes. His right shoe crushes Spider-Man's head. "It's not mom," he says. Then, surprising Michael: "And I'm sorry I poisoned you."

Michael thinks about Stephen's apology for a long moment. "It's okay," he finally says. "It's okay, Stephen. We're brothers, you know?"

"Yeah."

Michael hears his father and uncle downstairs: The rumbling trucks are laughing now. Laughing, perhaps, at dead and missing wives.

If I see the strange man in my dreams again tonight, Michael thinks, *I'll have to ask him about the letter. He seems like the kind of person who might know.*

It only takes Michael one try to get down the stairs because now he can concentrate. Now he can focus: fourteen steps.

Like the flies in his father's belly: in and down.

HOB

MICHAEL THINKS HOB is a fun name for the strange man. The man looks like a Hob, too. He has a long face and a goatee and very soft eyes. Michael thinks the man looks a little like his father.

Through the open window the crickets get quieter, and Michael sinks into the grey-black smudge of dreamland . . .

"Hello, Hob," Michael says.

Hob winks at Michael and waggles his eyebrows. "Ah, hello, Mr. Head. You've named me, have you?"

"Yes, Hob. Just as you've named me."

Hob taps his cane on the ground and smiles. "We're a couple of silly sods, aren't we? We in our queer suits and funny hats."

Michael discovers he has a cane too, this time. He taps it on the ground like Hob.

The background of the dream looks like someone has smeared charcoal across a piece of white paper. No other objects or people last night, but tonight there is a concrete bench off to the right of Hob. The bench is sticking out from nothing, held up by dream logic, and there's a young woman sitting on it, staring straight ahead at the empty grey space between Hob and Michael. She nods her head and laughs at something Michael can't hear.

"Who's that, Hob?" Michael asks.

"Who's who, Mr. Head? There's only you and me here, my boy." But Michael can tell Hob's lying. The woman makes Hob nervous.

Beneath the woman's laughter she seems very lonely and sad somehow—like she's waiting for someone she's pretty certain won't actually show up.

"You know about the letter I found today, don't you, Hob?" Michael says, and Michael knows he does, but he knows you can't trust everyone, so he wants to see if Hob lies to him, like he's lying about not being able to see the woman on the bench.

Hob simply nods once and lets his fingers melt nearly to the ground.

"Hello," Michael says to the woman. She ignores him.

"Who are you talking to, Mr. Head? I told you there's no one there." But Hob's fingers betray him—they twitch and flutter like flies against his cane.

Michael turns to Hob: "You're lying, you funny-looking man. You know she's there as well as I do."

Just because women don't exist in the real world, Michael thinks, *doesn't mean they can't exist in dreams.*

"You are as funny looking as I, Mr. Head; I thought we'd covered this topic quite thoroughly last night."

"What is she sad about, Hob?"

Hob turns his head away from Michael, pulls out his pocket watch, fiddles with it.

"Quit fiddling. You're just like my brother."

Hob sighs, strokes his goatee gently, finally looks up at Michael. His fingers snap up to his hand. "The letter. Okay, the letter. And the woman. You want to know about the letter and the woman."

"Well, you must be here for some reason, Hob. You can't be in my dream for nothing, can you? What would be the point of that?"

"Oh, so everything has to have a point, does it?" Hob says.

This is when the woman speaks:

"Hello," she says to Michael. "Do you have your mother's letter with you?"

"How do you know about my letter?" Michael asks.

Hob also turns to her. He looks at the woman on the bench

23

like he wants her to keep her mouth shut.

"Hob told me about it," she says, her voice the brittle bones of a small bird.

"What were you laughing at?" Michael asks the woman. She turns away from him, then, and stares again at the grey drabness around her.

"Oh, leave the poor woman alone, Mr. Head. Can't you see she's not interested in you?" Hob says.

Michael decides he needs to name the woman. Maybe with a name she'll talk to him.

"You have a very pretty face, and you deserve a very pretty name to go with it," Michael says, and takes a step toward her. Around him, the charcoal shifts and slowly settles again.

"Don't do too much of that moving around," says Hob. "There are secrets buried under this stuff. Things you don't want to know about."

"How about 'Marjorie'?" Michael asks, ignoring Hob's warning, but the woman only smiles faintly. The name feels wrong in Michael's mouth and he knows it's not good enough for her. He realizes then that he doesn't know many girls' names. His life is full of men, and that can be awfully tiring.

The only other girl's name he can think of is his mother's, so he tries that one out on her. "What do you think of 'Shirley'?"

She just laughs. Then Hob joins her and it's all a big joke.

Michael taps his cane on the ground a few times quickly, like a judge wanting order in his court, but they both keep laughing. Not hearty belly laughs, but tiny, polite laughter— enough to make Michael angry, but not enough to let him figure out *why* he's angry. And anger is no good in dreams; it only makes the dreamer powerless.

"Yes, very funny," Michael says. Then the name suddenly comes to him:

"Marla."

Hob and Marla both stop laughing.

Hob looks away, fidgeting with his cane while Marla turns to Michael, lips very red, very full. If Michael knew what a beautiful woman looked like, maybe she would be one.

"Can I see the letter, Mr. Head?" she says.

Michael pulls the letter from his pocket, unfolds it, hands it to Marla. Her hands match her voice—light, delicate. Michael waits for her eyes to go back and forth four times, the number of lines in the letter. Then he says, "My brother and I, we don't have a mom, Marla."

Hob whips out his pocket watch, shakes his head at the time, taps his cane twice. It's always getting late for Hob, always time to go. Michael wonders if there are even hands on his watch.

Marla says, "You used to have a mom, Mr. Head, but she left you, just like it says in the letter."

Marla folds the letter, looks up, sees Michael frowning, and laughs quietly again for a moment. Michael wonders what's so funny, but he's pretty sure he won't get any kind of straight answer, so he doesn't bother asking.

Hob doesn't join in the laughter this time; he's become very concerned with the hour. "I really should be off, Mr. Head."

"Goodbye, then, Hob." Michael is not in the mood for Hob's theatrics right now. He wants him to stop lying and acting twitchy. He wants him to join his cousins on the moon or wherever they are.

Hob tips his hat to Marla and Michael, mutters something under his breath. He walks away, kicking up very small clouds of charcoal.

Once he's out of earshot, Marla settles down a bit, asks Michael to sit next to her on the bench. She smells like candy canes, and it's then that Michael notices the glasses she's wearing—the frames are red-and-white striped, like candy canes. He smiles at this.

"So what did Hob offer you for the letter?" she asks Michael.

Michael's still thinking about candy canes and can only concentrate on inhaling her. "What is he supposed to have offered me?"

The contrast between Marla's sweet smell and the charcoal surrounding them, and the cold, is not lost on Michael—though he doesn't know why such a thing should matter. People dig and dig and put things inside him that he can't understand. It's been this way for as long as he can remember.

"Oh, I don't know; Hob offers people all sorts of things," Marla says. Her hair is long and wavy, auburn—the sort of hair, were he older, Michael might want to run his fingers through. He pictures himself doing this for a moment, but he feels Marla slipping away, her gaze wandering toward the endless landscape of charcoal around them. She cracks a smile and is about to start laughing at him again, so Michael thinks about baseball and frogs and frying ants with a magnifying glass and trading hockey cards with his brother and picking his nose, other silly kid stuff. Her expression sobers and she doesn't laugh.

Michael wonders, then, in what way Marla will love him, and, more importantly, if he'll approve.

"Well, what did Hob offer *you*, Marla?" Michael loves the way her name sounds, especially when his tongue makes the *L* sound against the roof of his mouth. "And for what?"

"I'm . . . waiting for someone, Mr. Head." Michael waits for her to go on, but she doesn't. She folds his letter up in her lap as small as it will go. There is only a certain number of times any piece of paper can be folded, but Marla folds and folds until the sheet is gone. When she can't fold the paper anymore, she folds her hands in her lap instead. Michael wonders if there is only a certain number of times a person can do that, too.

"What does that have to do with Hob?" Michael says.

"Hob says he can find the person I'm waiting for."

"Hob says a lot of things, Marla." And Michael feels so wise for saying this.

Marla folds her hands some more.

"What did you give him?" Michael asks, because he knows that everything has its price. That's what his father says, anyway, and fathers make their sons into whatever they want, so even if it's not true, he has been made to think it should be.

"Time," Marla says. "My time on this bench. It's his. His and that pocket watch he carries around." She looks at Michael very closely, then. Her eyes are green, a shade similar to Michael's suit. But where his suit is ugly, her eyes are not. Then he wonders if he would think that anyway, because he likes the way Marla smells and he likes Marla's voice and he likes her sundress, little patterns on it, little designs that he can't quite make out but doesn't want to because it might ruin the way she feels to him.

"How long have you been waiting, Marla?" Michael says, and suddenly feels himself waking up. She'll be gone soon and he doesn't know where his letter went. He feels panicked, like when he realized he'd drunk weed killer.

"I don't know," she answers. "A long time, I suppose. But maybe no time at all, since Hob has my time now. It's not really mine anymore, so I've sort of lost sense of it, you know?"

"Marla, can I have my letter back now? Where did it go?" And she's fading, Marla, the bench. Michael's nearly awake and hears cars whizzing by outside the window.

"Same place as the sticks, Mr. Head—under your hat."

Marla's voice crackles in Michael's ears as everything sinks to flat grey, washing out like watercolour. Then his arms are lifting his purple top hat from his head and the letter falls into his lap. He smiles at his Marla, which is how he's already come to think of her.

His.

And now another few questions tumble from his lips as two worlds blend, grey bench to white bunk-bed, Marla's bird bones to Stephen's quiet breathing: "Are there really secrets under the charcoal, Marla? Was Hob right? Was he telling the truth?"

"There are a few," she says, "but I don't know that they're nearly as dramatic as Hob makes them out to be, Mr. Head." The grey backdrop stutters and Marla is gone, but Michael still sees her face drifting around on his room's ceiling when he opens his eyes. She is laughing again.

Laughing and, Michael hopes, waiting for him to return.

HOME

GOING HOME. MICHAEL in the passenger seat, Stephen in the back, their father driving.

The car is fixed. Well, it runs, anyway. Calling it fixed would imply that nothing is wrong with it when there are, in fact, many things still wrong with it. But the thing that made Michael's father and uncle bend over it and crawl under it and curse at it and kick it is fixed.

For now.

But nothing is ever really fixed. Michael's father once told him about entropy and he never forgot. Something that depressing is hard to forget. Everything is eroding; people slow it down by fixing their cars and fixing their love lives and fixing their bodies, but in the end, it all falls apart anyway. Michael sometimes wonders how people get up every morning with this word waiting for them in every dictionary ever printed.

So there goes a cow, Michael thinks. *Zip. Moo. Bye, cow. We hardly knew you.*

So many cows in these fields. Michael wishes they would all start mooing at once. Then when they passed them he'd stick his head out the window and it would be like when a big truck is coming and it gets closer and closer, louder and louder, then it's to you, then it's past you: "mooooooooooOO OOOOOOOOooooooooooo!"

Cow rig, Michael thinks. *That would be funny.*

Anything would be better than listening to Stephen's dry sticks, and his father's boring organ music. It's all he ever plays.

Michael is scared that his uncle will find that the letter from the person who thinks she's his mother has been replaced with a blank sheet of paper. He'll know it was Michael; Stephen would be too stupid to have thought to replace it with another sheet of paper. His uncle knows this. Stephen would have just taken the letter and probably left the drawer wide open.

Clack, clack. There go the sticks again.

Moo, moo. As if in answer.

Cows and sticks. And Michael's uncle calling his father on the phone. *He's found the letter*, uncle will say. *Found it. Now he knows. He knows he has a mother. What are you going to do, brother? What are you going to do?*

Maybe father and uncle will kill Michael. Or maybe put him up in his uncle's attic with auntie. Sit him in her rotted lap. Make him kiss her maggoty lips, touch her sagging breasts. Sing songs to her. Who knows what fathers and uncles are capable of when cornered?

Another cow. Another clack. Stephen fiddles and fiddles and fiddles and fiddles and Michael's terrified there'll be a message about the letter on the answering machine at home, and he really wants to reach back and grab those sticks from Stephen's hands and snap them in two, because as much as Michael loves his brother, more than any father or mother or uncle or aunt could ever love him, he's scared and the letter feels big in his back pocket, he feels it expanding, growing, bursting through his jeans, and his father's looking over and asking, *What's that, son, where'd ya get that, son, ya little snooper, can't leave well enough alone, can ya, can ya, and now you know you have a mother, just like other kids, but you don't know where she is, you'll never know where she is*, but now here comes another cow and Michael rolls down the window and the cow saves the day because he moos *right at him*.

And the panic passes.

Just like that.

There're another few clacks from Stephen in the back seat, and Michael's heart pounds. But the letter is safe in his pocket. Small, contained—not big as a building.

Unseen. Unknown.

"Hello, cow," Michael says to another one as they pass it, slowing down to take a corner. The breeze from the open window dries his sweat. Another four lefts and one right and they're turning into their driveway.

Home.

The first thing Michael does is check for his mother in the attic.

❧ The stairs to Michael's attic are those pull-down kind. Stuffed up into the ceiling, and there's a bit of rope hanging that can be pulled to bring them down.

One time, a few years ago, Stephen sneaked up on Michael, watched him go up the stairs, then pushed them back in place once he was in the attic. No matter how hard Michael banged and shouted Stephen wouldn't let him out. After a few minutes of laughing, Stephen went back downstairs to the living room to listen to the radio. By the time their father got home, Michael was crying, curled into a ball on the cushionless couch stored there, trying to make up happy stories to keep away the dreadful feeling, which, from that day on, washed through him every time he even came near the attic stairs.

This time was no different, but Michael had to see if his mother was in the attic, rotting, like he thought auntie was in uncle's.

It's one of those old houses where everything's wired really strangely, so there's a switch down in the hallway to turn on the attic light. Michael flicks it. He pulls the stairs down, makes sure Stephen's not sneaking around anywhere, then climbs up. He just needs to take a quick look to be satisfied.

The air in the attic is always wet. Not just damp, but actually wet, like breathing water. When he reaches the top step, he notices that even the light seems wet. It ripples over the old couch in one corner, the paintings piled beside it, the dead bat in the other corner, the dilapidated card table no one ever used after his father bought it, and the stack of chairs lined up against the far wall, near the room's only window. Michael thinks this window is the coolest thing about the attic. Everything else is covered in dust, grime, filth from the ages, but the window is always clean. Spotless.

Michael stands at the top of the pull-down stairs and peers through the shadows and shifting pockets of watery light. Nothing on the couch. Nothing rotting beside the dead bat. Nothing stuffed under the chairs that he can see, and no legs poking out from behind the stack of paintings.

No body. No mother.

Then he hears someone coming up the third-floor stairs, fast. *If it's Stephen,* Michael thinks, *he'll—*

The light goes out. Michael's heart triple-kicks in his chest. Light fizzles above his head and the watery yellow filters away into the corners of the room.

Black. And very quiet laughter inside the walls around him.

Michael turns around and the stairs rise to meet him. They slam shut and he hears Stephen pull a chair across the hall, stand on it, and shove something in the slot near the pull cord to keep Michael from pushing the stairs down.

He did it again, Michael thinks. *I can't believe I'm this stupid. Why did I think he wouldn't do it to me twice? Because I cried the first time? So what? Stephen doesn't care. I'm a doofus. I will always be a doofus to him.*

Michael is already close to tears. He turns to the window, the window that is somehow always clean without anyone ever coming up here to clean it.

The last dribbles of sunlight squiggle out on the floor and the laughter in the walls thins out. Michael realizes he hasn't taken a breath since the light went out, so he does, and it's like soft earth filtering down his air pipe. He knows when he finally looks away from the window it will start. He already feels it weighing on his mind, pushing on his chest. It's what makes the walls laugh. It might even be what cleans the window. Like a dream, he can't do anything to stop it.

When he turns around, away from the window, it takes a few seconds for his eyes to adjust to the darkness in the corner where the couch is. It's pushing on his back, pushing him closer to the couch; it makes him step a few more feet, then holds him there, steadies his head. He feels it behind him, beside him, around him, but he knows it won't let him turn to see it because there would be nothing to see anyway. It's not a thing—it's the air itself. It coils around his legs and grips them, keeps his arms down by his sides, opens his eyes wider to see whatever it wants him to see on the couch.

He sees a bubble of white on one of the paintings near the arm of the couch. A hand. He follows the hand up to the arm, to the shoulder, to the floating face, and he's sure it's his dead mother. Her other hand is in her lap, curled tightly around the fabric of her dress. The dress looks washed of colour. She is black and white. The walls tell Michael that she is not dead, just gone away somewhere, but they don't say it in words, they just convey the emotion and Michael thinks it for himself because the walls are the air and the air is the thing that pushes him, holds him, lies to him, tries to make him see, make him know something he shouldn't know, something that can't be true: *Your mother is not dead. This isn't her, only your idea of her. Let this go. Let it go*, the lying walls say. And maybe he would, maybe he would try to let it go, but he sees her right here, sitting on this old attic couch.

Leering at him.

She hates him. He sees it in her eyes.

She relaxes her grip on her dress, then re-clamps her hand around the crumpled fabric, taps on the paintings, that white hand so much like Hob's, only not stretching but bubbling, and still tapping, and the leer splits her face like a busted jack-o'-lantern, and the air is thicker now and Michael's lungs are filling up fast and he feels the grip on his body crushing his bones. This thing that grinds him *knows* him, knows him better than any brother or mother or father; it knows his name, it has dug holes and has thrown things inside that don't belong, into everything that makes him who he is, just like everyone else in his life, and now his mother is staggering to her feet, her hands fluttering at her sides like butterflies, butterflies caught in bubbles, caught and dead in bubbles, and now the bubbles reach out to him, but the hate is still in her face, leaking from her split lantern skull, and she's saying, "I'm cold, I'm cold, where's your father, I'm cold, Michael," and he can't breathe, and she's still coming, and he's hitching in tiny gulps of air, too much soil, buried and drowning in it, too much and he can't—

The light comes on and Michael is only briefly able to close his eyes against it—one second, maybe two. Then they pop open again, shivers climb up his back, spread through his scalp, and his mother is standing directly in front of him.

"I'm cold, Michael," she hisses. "I'm cold. See?" And she touches his forearm with three of her fingers. "Tell your father that I'm very, very cold in here."

She pulls her fingers away from Michael's skin, but the cold stays. He looks down at the place on his forearm, then the next thing he knows the stairs are pulled down and his father is coming up them. He asks Michael if he's okay, what happened.

Michael does as he's told and passes on the message, even

though his mother's right there watching. He says, "Mom's cold, dad. Mom told me to tell you that she's really cold. You should do something about that if you can."

Michael brushes past his father and goes down the attic stairs to find Stephen. In an effort to control his anger toward his brother—scouting around outside for him, calling his name softly—he recalls the time Stephen saved him from drowning in the pool at their old house.

Laughing, playing, splashing, then water was in every part of him. Places where water shouldn't be, so he couldn't breathe. Michael sunk. His legs frozen. A stone. Plunk, right to the bottom. Outside sounds came to his ears through a thick blanket that he couldn't shake off. He remembers thinking: *Here I go. Now I die.*

Then a big splash and someone yanking on him, pulling hard. He breaks the surface and splutters, trying to pull in air—right then there is nothing of value but air in the whole universe. And then there's Stephen with his eyes open, looking down at Michael, who is on his back in the grass beside the pool.

So Michael thinks about this while he tracks Stephen down—to calm himself.

He creeps around the side of the house, and he hears Stephen before he sees him because of those sticks of his. Clatter-clack and there's his brother, sitting on a ratty old lawn chair, fiddling, fiddling.

"Why again, Stephen?" Michael says. "Why twice? You know how much it scared me the first time. You know."

"It's just an attic, Mikey," Stephen says.

Just an attic.

"Mom's up there, Stephen. I saw her. She told me to tell dad that she's cold." Michael pauses a second to see what his brother says, but Stephen's just looking at him.

"She's cold, Stephen," Michael says again.

The sticks stop, and something passes between these brothers. Stephen knows Michael's telling the truth, and for a tiny, tiny second they're poolside once more, Stephen with his wide-open eyes, saving Michael's life again. But mad at having to do it.

"How come this shit always happens to you, Mikey?" Stephen says.

"It doesn't matter, Stephen, and how come you're my own brother and I never call you 'Steve'?"

Michael drops his eyes and somehow this makes them even again.

But then this—this moment, this very instant, just when they're balanced again—this is when Stephen tells Michael he's found a second note from their dead mother.

✡ They're down in the basement and Stephen's showing Michael where he found the second letter.

"Right here," Stephen points. "Right in that crack in the wall. See it?"

Michael sees it, but he's not so sure he should tell Stephen that he sees it. "So it was just sticking out in plain sight?"

"No," Stephen says, takes a deep breath, holds it. Waits. Then: "No," he says again.

"Pretty buried in there, was it?" And it occurs to Michael again how no one around here does anything without being told.

"Yeah, pretty buried. Sort of, uh . . . folded, you know?"

"Lemme see it," Michael says.

Behind Michael are stairs; he doesn't know how many, though, because Stephen has never pushed him down these ones. The stairs are old, wooden, forever damp, like basement stairs always are.

Michael pulls the note from Stephen's hands and walks to the bottom of the stairs. The light from the landing allows him to read what's written:

Travelling. I've been travelling. Place to place. You know. Seeing things, seeing the world. Well, maybe not the world, but seeing a lot of North America, anyway. Meeting people. Interesting people. More interesting than you, that's for sure. More interesting than any of you. You think our lives have to be about kids, but why can't our lives just be about our lives? What's so wrong with that? I hope the boy is making you miserable.

That's note number two. Their dead or missing mother wishing them misery from parts unknown.

"Stuck in that crack right over there?" Michael asks, and points.

Stephen nods.

"Strange, huh?" Michael says.

Stephen nods again, but this time he talks, too: "Yeah, really weird. I came down to see if those old ice skates of mine were still down here, and I saw this hunk of white stickin' out a little."

Ice skates.

"What do you want with ice skates?" Michael asks his brother—his brother who has never been ice-skating in his life.

"I know I have a pair down here somewhere," Stephen says and looks around, down at his feet, over in the corner, beneath the stairs.

Michael wants very badly to call him a liar. He wants to say that this note isn't real, that the first one wasn't real, either, that their mother isn't missing, that the whole situation is non-existent. He would very much like to be able to say and believe these things.

But he can't.

The handwriting is the same. The notes match. Their mother wrote home again about a year after she left.

Then Stephen says something completely stupid and Michael knows he has to go up the stairs, away from his brother. He knows he must get as far away from him as he can right now. Stephen says, "Pretty cool to have a mom again, huh?"

For a fast second, the room tilts, and Michael has to sit down on the bottom stair. In a quick, red flash, he sees Stephen's head crushed to a blurred streak on the basement floor, and he tries to remember how Stephen once saved his life. His brother, with his annoying sticks and *Spider-Man* comic books, saved his life that day at the old pool. He is responsible for the air in Michael's lungs; he is the reason Michael has to even bother trying to control his anger at his brother right now.

"We don't have a mother," Michael says, looking at his shoes. The laces are untied. He might trip and kill myself, break his neck, shatter his spine, crack his skull. "No mom, Stephen. These are letters," Michael says.

Michael looks up at Stephen, most of the anger gone. "Just letters. From a long time ago."

MARLA

MICHAEL IS ASLEEP again. He sits on the bench and stares at the spot where he'd been standing when Hob told him he should be careful about stirring up secrets. He stares long and hard, and his eyes burn.

He has no idea where Hob is, no idea where Marla is.

Where do people from your dreams go, Michael thinks, *when they're not in your dreams?*

He feels a soft hand on his shoulder. He blinks, droplets fall from his eyelids, disappear into the grey at his feet. He turns his head slowly, and Marla is wiping his eyes, smiling.

"Where were you?" he asks, returning her smile, tasting salt as the tears find his top lip.

"Oh, here and there. You know."

"Aren't you waiting for that person anymore?"

"Yes, but sometimes Hob lets me go. He knows how boring it can get, and he does have a heart . . . though a very hard one. Like a chestnut."

Michael smiles wider. "So where *is* Hob, anyway?"

"Fiddling with things," she answers and looks away.

Michael reaches down and finds Marla's fingers. He holds onto them tightly. It's awkward, and he thinks he might be blushing, but she doesn't pull away and they're both still smiling, so it can't be a bad thing.

"You know something," Marla says, and there's her voice again. Soft. "You're sort of like the person I'm waiting for, I think. Though I'm not sure how I would know that since I don't even know myself who I'm waiting for."

Michael blinks and waits. Squeezes her hand.

"But you're too young to be him. The man I'm waiting

for—you would think it's a man, wouldn't you?—would have to be at least thirty by now, maybe even forty. Or that's how it feels anyway. Like I said, I've been waiting a long time. Hob knows exactly how long, too—he keeps track with that watch of his—but he won't tell me, no matter how often I ask. Come to think of it, maybe he's just been lying to me all along, and he knows how long I've been here only as well as I do, which is not at all.

"I asked him, once," Marla continues, "if I could see his watch. He said, 'What watch?' and stuffed it into one of his big pants pockets. He smiled at me, all innocent, and I just wanted to sock him one."

Marla laughs, and Michael laughs, and the charcoal shuffles a little, but not enough to reveal anything. Not that Michael thinks there's really anything under there. At least nothing to be afraid of.

Before he can stop himself, right after they're done laughing, Michael says, "Marla, are you dead?" His heart whacks against his chest. "I mean, is the person you're waiting for dead?"

Marla keeps smiling. Michael's heart settles a little.

"I don't think so, Mr. Head. To either question. But I don't think I would care in either case. When you're waiting for someone, you're just . . . waiting for them, you know?" And she smiles at Michael again. Squeezes his hand.

He is so simple, and she is so simple. The relationship they have is perfect. They sit, holding hands in his dream, and he finds himself wishing desperately that she were real.

A REAL SLICE OF HEAVEN

MICHAEL WAKES UP and today is like any other day, like any other day that ever was. Michael thinks that people who've been raped and killed used to wake up the same way he does each morning. People who hate their lives and would like nothing better than to just die quickly wake up just like this. Tired, faintly hungry, and waiting for the pool guys to show up.

So what, Michael imagines his father thinking, *if my youngest son nearly drowned in the last pool we had? Pools are a barrel of monkeys. Pools beat anything. When you say the word* pool *to a person—especially on a really hot, sticky day—their eyes tell the whole story. Pools are wonderful.*

Yes, dad, it's true, Michael thinks. *Pools are a real slice of heaven.*

So here they come, the pool guys, barrelling up the street. Even just strapped down and being pulled by a truck, that big excavator thing is terrifying. Its giant claw digging dirt.

You could stuff about fifty screaming babies in the claw of one of those things, Michael thinks. *Maybe sixty.*

With all the excitement of the new pool coming, Michael's really close to forgetting about Marla, Hob, the new letter from his dead mother, and all that other stuff. Won't it be fun to try and drown again?

Michael gets out of bed, walks down the stairs, through the front door, and out onto his searing-hot driveway. He's barefoot and feels his soles sizzling.

Stephen walks up behind him, and Michael hears his brother's sticks going full tilt already. Too early in the morning to be that fidgety. Michael wonders what Stephen could possibly be nervous about. *He* was the one who almost died in the last pool they had. Michael thinks maybe Stephen's just afraid he'll have to save him again.

Michael turns around, steps onto a different patch of tarmac. More sizzling: fresh filet of sole. "Where's dad?" he asks.

Stephen fiddles with his sticks, looks over his shoulder, hypnotized by the approaching parade of heavy yellow things. "Here comes the pool," he mumbles. His lips are chapped; he sucks on them between words.

"Yeah, here it comes," Michael agrees, like it's just this big, ready-to-dive-into pool.

One more try.

"Do you know where dad went, Stephen?"

Stephen mumbles something else and walks away from Michael.

Michael takes a deep breath, holds it.

"Hey, kid, your mom or dad around?"

Michael turns, exhaling, and there's a big black guy leaning out of the truck that's brought the giant dirt-digging claw.

"My mom is dead," Michael says, "or at the very least missing. And I just asked my brother where my dad was, but he walked away from me."

And here comes his father, walking up the driveway, plastic 7-Eleven bag in his hand. Michael knows his father does not like black men, so he decides to stand around and see what happens.

"Dad," Michael says. "Pool's here."

Michael steps back three paces. Just enough for his father to forget about him.

Michael sees it when his father lifts his head toward the man in the truck. His eyes harden and his face muscles drop. He is disgusted but is showing only the hard inner nugget of that disgust. He's really not such a bad guy. He just sees differences everywhere. He's on high alert for them, and when he catches one, he's all over it, will rip at it, tear at it, trap it like fifty screaming babies in a giant yellow claw until it understands that it is unwanted, that there is something wrong with it.

"You come to do the hole for the pool?" says Michael's father.

"Yep," says the truck guy.

"Right. Get to it, then." Michael's father walks away.

Michael looks at the face of the truck guy, and sees that he knows. He knows that Michael's father hates him. He looks back at Michael, smiles. "Dead or missing, huh? You don't know which?"

"Nope," Michael says, and shrugs.

The first guy gets out of the truck; another black guy gets out of the other side of the cab. Now there are two black men on their property. Michael thinks that his father would handle it better if there were one white guy and one black guy, though he would think less of the white guy for keeping such company.

"Doesn't seem to bother you too much, kid," the first guy says.

"Why should it? Either way she's gone."

The first guy's smile slips for a second, then slides back onto his face. His teeth are very white, and his eyes are very soft. He nods and laughs a little, moves to the back of the truck with his partner.

Michael walks back into the house for some breakfast, wondering what was funny.

DIGGING

THEY DIG AND they dig and they dig and then there's a head poking out. A skull saying hello from the Other Side. Gazing up through dirt, grinning. Black worker number two discovers it, starts shrieking, then runs to get black worker number one. Number One takes a look at it and throws up in the bushes. Apparently there is still some skin and crawling things on it.

The boys' father comes out of the house to see what's up. He takes one long look at the discovery and everyone's overreacting 'cause it turns out it's not a human skull.

The skull was only half uncovered, and maybe Number Two's been watching too many scary movies and thought he saw the face of The Devil Himself staring up from the dirt. But it's just a dog's head, probably attached to the rest of its body farther across in the earth.

The boys' father kicks the dog's head and says, "It's just a dog; get back to work."

But it's late anyway, and Number Two's too shaken from his encounter with the Devil Dog to continue working. Michael sees that Number One, with his shiny teeth and warm, soft eyes, is embarrassed by his partner and even more embarrassed about himself, and just wants to go home. If Hob were here, he'd have set them all straight with his warning about being careful not to disturb the ground. Things that should stay hidden and all that.

The Number Brothers start packing up—Number Two dropping things twice and three times, his hands are so shaky— and promise to bring a couple more Numbers tomorrow to help with the rest of the job. The boys' father storms off, slams the back door.

Michael turns around because he feels like someone's watching him, and there's Stephen standing in their bedroom window, looking down at the decaying dog's head.

Just standing there, staring.

The Number Brothers wave at Michael and he waves back. *Good guys*, Michael thinks. *Solid workers. But so what if it had been a human head in their yard? Probably just someone's dead mother anyway.*

BURYING

THERE'S A MAN who comes in the night and buries things in the boys' backyard. Stephen says he saw him. He says he saw him bury the dog about a week ago.

"Why would someone dig holes and leave things in our yard, Stephen?" Michael asks. Stephen's standing in the same position he was when Michael had been outside and had looked back and saw him in their window. Only now Michael can't see his brother's face.

"You don't have to believe me, doofus, but I saw him."

"What did he look like, Stephen?" Michael says.

"Couldn't see him that well. It was dark and he was wearing—"

"Stephen, can you face me when we're talking?"

Stephen turns around slowly. There's something in his eyes now. Not hate, but frustration. He doesn't like it when Michael makes him acknowledge the fact that he's talking to his brother.

"Dark clothes," he finishes. "He was wearing dark clothes."

"Did you see him in a flash of lightning, Stephen?" Michael asks. "Like in the panel of a comic book?"

Stephen turns his back on Michael again. "I saw him bury that dog, Mikey. You don't have to believe me."

And he's right, Michael doesn't. But he wants to. He really, really wants to.

"I'm sorry, Stephen. Tell me what he looks like."

Stephen continues staring out the window. Michael knows his brother is going to make him say please. Apologies aren't what he wants. Apologies mean nothing to him. They never have.

But Michael wants to know. Michael wants to know what the man who buries dead dogs in their backyard looks like. Even if he doesn't exist. So he says it. He says, "Please."

Stephen is quiet for a few more seconds. Taking in the moment. Lathering himself in Michael's need.

"I don't know. Just black, Mikey. He was short and wearing black. That's all I really saw. And he dug. Dug that dog a hole and plopped it in."

"What else has he buried, Stephen?" Michael asks, playing along.

"Just dogs," Stephen says. "Nothing but dogs." His back is still turned.

Michael is trying to understand why his brother is saying these things; he's trying to understand what's in it for Stephen to tell him these lies. But he thinks of nothing. So Michael asks him: "Why just dogs, Stephen? Why not other animals or people or treasure?"

Stephen says to the window: "Are those pool guys coming back tomorrow?"

Michael says nothing, because he knows they are.

"Tomorrow they'll find another dog," Stephen says, and walks past Michael out of their bedroom, closes the door, walks across the hall, into the spare room. Where, of course, he has another set of sticks. As soon as he sits down on the bed, the sticks start.

His life is fiddling with sticks, reading comic books, and telling lies.

His sticks are clacking through the closed door—some rhythm Michael almost senses. Something like a message. Then he changes the pattern and Michael can't keep up.

Michael walks across the hall, into the spare room, sits next to Stephen. He hears his father downstairs. He must be talking on the phone to his brother because he's laughing in that way that he only laughs with his brother. Guarded.

Michael is looking at Stephen, who's looking at his sticks. Michael leans in close to him, the pressure of his hand on the bed releasing the smell of the sheets. The smell of spare. The smell of No One Ever Sleeps Here.

And now he's saying something very quietly into Stephen's ear, his lip against his brother's lobe. Stephen doesn't move away from Michael, doesn't stop his sticks. Won't stop those sticks for anything.

So Michael asks him his question, the thing he needs to know: "Why don't I see the same things you see, Stephen?"

The answer is so soft, so measured, and it's timed to the rhythm of Stephen's clacking: "Because you don't want to see them, Mikey. You don't want to know."

Michael pulls his head away from Stephen and stares for a while at his brother's lips. Those lips that have finally said something meaningful.

Then he gets off the bed quietly, walks across the hall again, climbs into his bunk, and closes his eyes.

GOD

IN MICHAEL'S DREAM that night, Hob is a great and terrible god. His head is huge, and that's all there is. It hovers over the charcoal landscape, looks down with disapproval. If he wasn't just a big head, he would be tapping something, or looking at his pocket watch, counting down the seconds until the end of this world. Because that's what it feels like to Michael when he looks up into the eyes of Hob's giant head. The end of everything he has control over. The end of the grey, the end of Marla's bench. The end of Marla.

Hob's eyes do not burn with any sort of fury, like you'd expect proper god's eyes to do. They're just two dull, dirty coins in his pale, pasty face. Flat, emotionless, without reason.

Nothing can die here, his eyes say, as he sweeps his dull coins from one side of the horizon to the other. His voice is a mountain. Michael's sure he would like to think it's some forbidden mountain where None Shall Pass. But it's just a loud noise; it's just a gorilla beating its chest with loose fists and limp wrists.

There is no reason to be afraid, his eyes continue. Michael hears Hob's pocket watch ticking, ticking, and that's far more unsettling than anything else in this show. *But I can take it all away. Young boys and the funnymen with no tongues will show you: The clock stops not in the heart, but lower. Deeper.*

And he's so mysterious, our Hob. Riddle us; tell us of this Death in the Belly. Stump us with your divine wisdom. Today Michael is also a god, and gods and showmen don't hold their cards very close to their vests. You see them coming a mile away. They are beyond obvious. Gods especially. They have rules. You must obey the rules. If you do not obey the rules, something bad will happen to you. It's not very complicated. It's not very mysterious at all. They bluster and they preen and make it all about them.

A god is just a regular person, Michael thinks, *but with a head as far as the eye can see.*

Michael opens his mouth to tell Hob he's not scared of his head. He opens it to tell Hob that despite the size of his head and mountainous voice, he will always be a small man with an ugly suit and a funny hat.

When Michael does finally open his mouth, when his vocal cords—the air in his lungs, his lips, tongue, and teeth—start to churn up the sounds that are to create his words, he feels his head expanding, stretching, growing huge; the cords in his throat hardening, growing tips, points, peaks; they become massive triangles of Threatening Power.

And here come the words. Here comes the fury. Flames burst out of Michael's eyeballs, singe his eyebrows, scorch the skin above the sockets, like they're the shattered windows of a gutted house. He is as devastating as anything in creation, and he is about to speak.

Hob's face remains flat, calm. Now his eyes simply say, *You will not win.*

And Michael thinks, *I will not win.*

And that's all it takes, because Michael is a coward. The words die in his throat; the flames in his eyes wink out, turn to stitched black Xs through which he can barely see. He is small again, a little boy asleep, dreaming, afraid to believe in something more powerful than himself.

The head above him, all around him, throbs, pulses, pumps with life. The ticking of the pocket watch grows louder in his ears until it is thick slabs of rock falling one on top of another, piling high. The End of All Worlds.

In the distance, at ground level, the charcoal swirls, grey

streaks whipping up in front of the giant head of Hob the Terrible. He does not smile. He does not waggle his eyebrows. He is trying to tell Michael something important, but Michael's not listening very closely. Gods need to be heard. Gods need attention.

You will not win, his eyes say again. *This is the end of your world.*

Then the grey streaks turn to thick clouds. Higher and higher into the nothingness above Michael, columns of charcoal dust twist around each other until the giant head is obscured, and only the flat black of its watching eyes bleeds through the perfect wall of grey.

And it's coming closer.

The wall gets thicker; the shaking ground in front of Michael gets smaller, somehow thinner. It's being torn up like carpet. The great, fat head edges closer.

X marks the spot. Beneath is the treasure. Two Xs, two treasures. Michael raises his hands to his face and starts digging.

God has beaten him. He digs past the Xs in his eyes and slithers inside to hide, terrified.

God has won.

God always wins.

There is a bright flash, just barely reaching Michael where he sits huddled in a corner of his skull.

There is no treasure under the Xs. There never is.

The flash repeats, this time brighter, and he's suddenly sitting next to Marla on their bench. The charcoal ground beneath them remembers nothing.

Michael sees a normal-size Hob coming from a long way off. He's a little green dot against the surrounding grey surface. At first he seems to be floating toward them, but then Michael sees his legs like scissors, then like long, thin spider legs, creeping along. His cane taps the ground with each step, tiny puffs of grey swarming around the bottom of it as he gets closer.

Marla and Michael hold hands and say nothing as they watch him.

The grey around them darkens a little when Hob takes his last few steps. Marla and Michael try to look away, anywhere but at Hob. But he positions himself right in front of them, smiling broadly; the double tap of his cane on the bench between them gets their attention.

"I have a surprise for you today, Mr. Head," Hob says, his free hand tapping his chin lightly. "Yes, a surprise," he says, and winks.

Michael says nothing. Marla grips his hand a little tighter. Things have changed. Hob has gone from an annoyance to someone holding more than just a tiny bit of threat.

But this is still my world, Michael thinks. *Still my dream.*

Michael wants to spend time with Marla. He thinks that if he dreams about her every night for a very long time she will become more and more real, until he can't tell whether he's asleep or awake.

"Would you like that, Mr. Head?" Hob says. Michael expects him to wink again because that's what he does. He taps his cane, says silly things, and winks. But he doesn't wink this time, just waits for Michael's answer. That's the thing about Hob. Just when you think—

And he taps his cane again. Michael's mind is wandering and he knows it. Marla stares at Hob's feet. She stares and thinks about why the person she's waiting for won't come. Why the person she's waiting for is taking so long to—

And there's Hob's cane again. Harder this time. Grey swirls and settles, swirls and settles, and before Michael's mind can stray again, Hob says, "A surprise, what do you think? Answer me, what do you think? Answer me now."

Michael looks up and Hob's face is flat. No winking, no smiling. He's losing his grip and he knows it.

Michael's mind is his own. It's his, and—

The cane snaps against Michael's thigh. Marla lets go of Michael's hand, puts both of hers up to her face and starts crying. Michael doesn't feel the pain from the contact, but he feels his eyes grow very hard in his skull. He knows he's glaring at Hob.

Gods need to be heard, listened to.

"Surprise. Surprise. It will be fun. Come along."

"You hit me, Hob," Michael says.

"A surprise," he says, and whacks Michael again, harder.

"What is the surprise, Hob?"

"A carnival, Mr. Head. Just for you and your lady friend."

"Her name is Marla, Hob. You know her name is Marla."

"A carnival," he says again, and his smile returns. "A carnival for you and your *lady* friend."

When Michael frowns at this, it feels like his face is made of dry plaster, and it cracks, pieces falling to the ground around him, bits striking the bench and cracking into even smaller bits. Someone else's face is under Michael's. He raises his arms and feels the nose, cheekbones, lips. They're not his.

"Whose face?" Michael asks, and Hob just winks.

"You are legion," he says, and laughs.

And because Michael feels as though he is still himself, not this new-face person, he says something that only he would say. He says, "I will go to the carnival if you give me different clothes to wear. I don't want to look like you anymore."

"You can wear whatever you like, Mr. Head. No one ever forced you to wear those clothes to begin with. What would you like, then?" Hob lights one of his long cigarettes and slips it between his lips, puffs twice. "A pair of sheep pyjamas? Maybe penguins? No, no, what about squirrels? Yes, I think squirrel pyjamas would go over quite well at the carnival. Many animals will be in attendance, and I'm sure they'll all appreciate the gesture."

"I want to wear my own clothes," Michael says, and Marla has stopped crying and has gone back to staring at Hob's feet. Michael tries to take her hand, but when he reaches for it, she moves it away.

"I want blue jeans and a regular T-shirt. I want to be me at the carnival." Michael thinks of his face again, reaches a hand up to explore its alien features. Angry, he brushes plaster pieces off his lap onto the ground.

Hob laughs a little. "You can't be yourself, Mr. Head; no one can be who he really is at the carnival. Not this one, anyway. This carnival is make-believe. It's for dressing up and playing the part!"

"What part?"

"Why, any part but your own, Mr. Head. Any part but your own." Hob reaches into his pocket and pulls out his watch. Slabs of rock falling on each other as the seconds tick by. "Now come, we'll be late. We must hurry. Rouse your lady friend and we'll be off." He puts the watch away and flexes his spider legs, limbering them up for the walk ahead.

But Michael feels he needs to cling to this. He needs to be himself at this carnival. He already wears someone else's face; he can't wear someone else's clothes, too. He won't know what to do or how to act if he's not himself.

Memories of the carnival to which his father takes him and his brother sift into his mind. Panic nestles in his chest.

Hob taps his cane once more, as though he's come to a decision, spins to his left and walks away.

Michael is trying to think of anything except this. He's

trying with everything he has left inside him to think of anything but what he's thinking right now. But he can't stop it, and Marla isn't helping at all because she's still just staring at the place where Hob's feet used to be, and she won't let Michael hold her hand, and Michael can't look at her with his eyes because they aren't his eyes anymore, and she won't look at him because he's lost who he is, and he's ashamed because he did it right in front of her, right in front of his Marla, the only one who loves him like she should, the only one who knows that the thought he's thinking right now—the thought that won't leave the head that is *not* his head—isn't his thought at all, but he can't stop thinking it, he can't stop thinking the thought, the thought is:

Follow the spider.

He looks up to see Hob walking slowly, getting smaller, becoming that green speck again. Marla is still beside him. Very gently, she touches his hand, and it crumbles. He looks down and it's not his hand. It's older. Bigger. Wrinkled. Aged.

Michael stands up to (*follow the spider*) think about the carnival. To just *think* about whether he should go. Suddenly, he starts walking. Hob's footsteps in the charcoal are easy to make out, so Michael follows in them. Their shoes are exactly the same size.

Michael thinks: *Will there be rides to go on at the carnival? What will the animals think of me if I'm not wearing squirrel pyjamas? How can someone guess my weight if I'm not me anymore? What will I tell them? I can't lie about something like that; they'll know and then they'll not ask me back to the carnival again. Though I'm not sure why I should care about that. But then, I'm not me anymore, so what does it matter? It will all be on someone else's mind.*

Michael follows Hob's footsteps, becomes a small speck just like he did. That's when he remembers Marla, still back there sitting on the bench, probably wondering where he's going and who he's become.

But Michael doesn't have to worry because she's not back on the bench, she's suddenly right beside him, walking, picking off plaster pieces of him and holding his new hand, telling him it will be okay, that she's been to the carnival before and it's not so bad.

She's picking and she's picking, and Michael asks, "What clothes am I wearing, Marla? What's underneath the plaster?"

But Marla is busy discovering him, and she doesn't answer, just keeps repeating that she's been to the carnival and it'll be okay, not to worry.

She's smiling, Marla is smiling, so it can't be so bad, Michael thinks. But now Marla's crying right through her smile. A chunk of Michael's shoulder comes off in her hand and she cries harder while it crumbles.

I'm falling apart, Michael thinks, and it's the clearest thought he's had since he got here tonight.

Falling to pieces and following the spider to the carnival.

DOGS

FIVE BLACK MEN in Michael's backyard. He can't believe it. And Michael's father himself, tight-lipped, drinking tea and watching them from the kitchen window. Watching them very, very closely.

The Number Brothers came back with three others today, and they're going at it hard in the sun. They all have their shirts off and there's all that black skin out there. A vein in Michael's father's head looks ready to burst.

It doesn't matter to Michael what colour hands dig the hole for the pool. It's the pool Michael thinks he's going to drown in. Some people were made to be accountants, others teachers, still others famous radio show hosts. But not Michael—he was made solely to drown in pools. That's all he has to look forward to and it's not going to be long now. Michael thinks his father knows he's going to drown, but he's still going to build this pool. And this time, he'll make sure Stephen's not around to save Michael.

Michael wonders if it's the flies in his father's belly making him do this.

Right when his father starts washing out his teacup—water swirling, the hiss of the tap—that's when one of the Number Brothers walks up to the sliding glass door that looks out on the backyard. He knocks lightly on it, looking very sheepish, concerned.

Michael's father is already scowling, mumbling under his breath. He unlocks the door, swings it open, letting hot air in.

"Yes," he says to the Number Brother. Not a question, like he knows whatever it is this man is going to tell him, it's going to be ridiculous, just like the dog yesterday. A waste of time and money.

"We found another one, sir," says the guy.

"Another what?"

"Dog. We found another dead dog."

Michael's father curses and storms out into the yard, leaving the door open. Michael follows, like the shadow of his father that he is.

Then there's the dog's head and half of its body, poking out of the soil, just like the last one. Partially decayed. This dog looks a bit smaller than the last one, though. But there's something not like the other dog: this one has a piece of paper stuck to its jaw, sort of plastered against it. Brown. So dirty it can barely be seen. Could be anything—strip of newspaper, piece of a magazine, page of a book—but it's not. It's a note.

Michael looks at his father and then at the Number Brothers, all standing around looking confused, disgusted.

"Well, pull it out and trash it. Same as the last one," Michael's father says and stalks back into the house. But Michael knows even his father has to be wondering where these dead dogs are coming from. He just doesn't want to look out of control in front of the Numbers. You have to control them. That's what his father thinks. Controlling them is what makes you better than them. But his father is gone in the house now, and Michael's left with the Numbers.

Michael keeps watching them, expecting one of them to notice the muddied note stuck to the dog's jaw, pull it off, read it, spoil everything, but no one does. They just start digging around the rest of its body and yanking the pieces out, stuffing them in a big, green garbage bag.

Right where he knew he'd be, Michael turns around and there's Stephen on the second floor, at their window again, looking down. He knows what they found—he knew it before they'd even dug their shovels in for the day. But only Michael and his brother know about the man who comes in the middle of the night to their yard to bury dead dogs. Everyone else is confused, powerless.

How can Michael not believe Stephen now? He said the Numbers would find another dog, and they have. Michael looks down at the ground and wonders how many more are hidden under there. A carpet of dead dogs?

Michael watches the Numbers put the second dog's remains in a metal garbage can. They don't know it, but Michael does: garbage day is tomorrow, so Michael has to get that note back tonight when everyone leaves.

The note is from the boys' mother. Michael knows that. Of course, he wonders why it's smeared into a dead dog's face, buried in their backyard—but then he wonders about the strange place Stephen found the second note, too.

He and his brother have found one each, but Michael knows that this one is intended for him. His mother wants to tell him something. Maybe she's going to tell him where she is, or at least what happened to her. Michael breaks out in a sweat thinking about what could be inside the letter, the words written there. It can't be some discarded, meaningless piece of scrap paper. Maybe it could have been at first, before Michael had started thinking about it, but now it's too late—now it's a special message just for him.

Her son.

Walking back to the sliding door, Michael thinks that this will be the last letter, the one that explains everything. He's so glad Stephen didn't find it. Stephen has too much control anyway. He knows things—like the stuff about the dogs in their yard—that he has no right knowing, and that makes Michael jealous.

Stepping out of his muddy shoes when he gets in the door,

Michael already hears Stephen's sticks clacking away upstairs. Stephen doesn't want to know about the letter, but Michael's going to tell him. Stephen told Michael about the second one when he didn't want to hear about it, so now it's his turn. If nothing else, Michael wants his relationship with his brother to be fair.

When Michael climbs the stairs and walks into their room, Stephen has both letters from their mother out and is staring down at them in his hands. The sticks have stopped because Stephen likes to be fair, too.

"Where was it?" Stephen says, not looking up.

"On the jaw. Plastered there," Michael says.

Stephen nods. "You know," he says, "this note won't be for you. You might think it is 'cause you found it, but it's not." He finally looks up at Michael. "It's not," he repeats.

"It was stuck to the dog's jaw, Stephen. No one else saw it. I'll bet even if you'd been right there beside me you wouldn't have seen it either. And you know it."

Suddenly things aren't very fair any more. Michael doesn't know how to stop things when they get like this. Neither does Stephen, and so they play them out every time.

"The first two notes weren't for you," Stephen says. "What makes you think this one will be? Besides, who told you it was going to be found? Who told you—"

But that's not what Stephen told Michael, that's not what he told him at all, and Michael's going to say that, say it right to his brother's face, he says, "You didn't say that. You didn't *say* we'd find a note; you said the Number Brothers would find another dead dog. And you were right about that, yeah, but only because you happened to see the guy who digs holes and puts the dogs in our yard. But just because you see him, just because of that, it doesn't mean you know where mom's next note is going to be, it doesn't mean that at all."

Michael is defiant. He is raging. He is arguing with his brother over notes from their dead mother, because he realizes that he wants it all to be true. It feels wonderful to be *able* to argue over a mother—who she loves most, who she's coming back for, and when it will be, what she'll look like, what colour eyes she has, and why she left them in the first place. The last part of that should be the most important, but it's really not. Michael doesn't care why she left; it's enough to know that she's coming back.

But she's not.

Michael knows it and Stephen knows it, but they don't know it where it really counts. They know it in their minds, but not in their hearts. In their hearts she's real, and she's coming, and she's leaving notes for them, and she'll return soon and love them properly.

Stephen says, "We don't even know for sure that it's from her."

But his words hang in the air like a word bubble from one of his comic books. They aren't real. It's almost silly to even think about it.

"It's from her, Stephen," Michael says.

Michael walks out of the room, feeling Stephen's eyes on his back. He has some time to kill before the Numbers finish their work for the day and he's free to go get the note out of the garbage. It's Stephen's day to go find more sticks in the woods behind their house—he goes out for new ones about once a month—so Michael decides to go up to the attic again to see if his mother's still there. Michael knows there's nothing he can do to make her warmer, but maybe she can tell him something about the flies and what they've done with his aunt.

Michael knows deep down inside that whatever his mother decides to tell him, if she decides to speak at all, it's going to be a message for Stephen or their father. Michael is here, she sees him, but she doesn't recognize him. For some reason that he does not understand, he does not exist to her.

But he's certain that if he and Stephen can find some more dead dogs with notes from dead mothers in their yard everything will work out okay. Their mother will come home for real, Stephen will stop playing with his sticks, their father will stop eating flies, and Michael will stop hoping for all of this to come true.

✿ The house is silent. Michael hears his father outside, mowing the front lawn. The Numbers are working hard out back. Somewhere in the woods, Stephen is collecting more sticks to clatter together, more noise to shield himself from the world.

Michael has gone up into the attic without turning on the light. He wants to be in that complete blackness that makes anything possible. Maybe this time his mother will say something for him. Maybe she'll say the kinds of things Marla says to him. He would like to feel that way when he's awake and it's actually happening to the real him. He wants something to feel and hold onto tightly—something he knows wasn't created by his own mind.

Outside the light is failing and he hears muffled shouts and heavy machinery being moved around to the front of the house. The Numbers are calling it a day.

Michael stares at the old couch in the attic. The one where his mother was sitting. He stares for a good five minutes.

Michael turns his head; the light coming in from the window that somehow cleans itself is grey. Grey turning to black with each breath he takes. It's like the shutter on a camera when he blinks, the light fading fast, nearly gone.

Now dark. Just starlight in the window, and the small noises of the Numbers rumbling away down the street.

He turns back to the couch. Still no mother. Still no floating white hand tapping the tops of the paintings. Just silence as his father turns off the mower and comes inside. Michael hears the flies buzzing, welcoming his father home.

"Mom?" Michael whispers.

He thinks about how stupid he is. *Mom can't be here, she can't be dead. She wrote those letters, the letters that will eventually say how she's coming back soon, that she's on her way.*

His father's taking the garbage out. Michael hears him slam the metal can onto the curb out front. Then, straight after that noise, another one, this one closer. Right behind him. Glass tinkling, ever so softly.

He turns around fully, facing the window. There are lights in the window. Glowing lights. Flashing lights. Jumping lights.

And now voices, too. Trapped in a can. Trapped in the window.

He steps forward, closer to the frame, only a few feet away now; closer still and the window is all he sees.

Music. Carnival music. Men shouting. The lid on the can opens and he hears their voices clearer now.

This carnival is like the one to which the boys' father takes them. The kind of carnival where the farther in you go, the more you feel like you're sinking into the ground. Reality falls away as the lights and the motions and the noises blend into a downward spiral where you forget your name, forget what the outside world is like.

Where you forget how to remember.

Michael has no idea whether he's asleep or awake, but he sees Hob in the window, easy to spot in his green suit and top hat, his spider walk. He's weaving between the people, between their canned voices. The voices take shape and these are carnival-goers, kids with cotton candy, tall, skinny men bellowing about guessing people's weight, giant men banging giant hammers, trying to ring a giant bell. It's all about size at carnivals. It's about size, and it's about that feeling of dread you get when you think the actor playing the part of the clown isn't acting.

Hob's talking with someone down there, pointing up to one of the rides, laughing, clapping the man on the back. He's smoking one of his never-ending cigarettes and it's fogging up the lower-right quarter of the window frame.

Michael wonders where Marla is. He doesn't see her with Hob. He scans the crowd for her dress, her smile, but there's nothing. No one even looks close to her. No one is even wearing a dress. He keeps scanning and then realizes there are no women in the crowd. They're all men.

Men and animals.

And all Michael thinks is: *I have to find her. I have to find her. No time for ghosts who might never show up, I have to find Marla. She's there, at the carnival; she's got to be. Unless the person she was waiting for finally showed up and has taken her away, taken her away from me, and I'll never see her again, my Marla, her hand, the warmth of her hand, her soft eyes, and someone has stolen her, someone at this carnival has her, I have to find her, I need to be—*

—here . . . in the carnival.

It's bright; it's loud. Michael is suddenly somehow inside. He has followed the spider to the carnival.

But he's awake. He knows he's awake. He's still breathing the thick attic air, but he sees a sea of men and boys. The men all look old, rotted, wet, and limp—dragging themselves along, weak smiles on their wrinkled faces; the boys all seem to shine. Some of their smiles are blinding.

Just ahead of Michael, Hob's back is turned, his arm still around the man he had been clapping on the back and laughing with. All around Michael is laughter and vacant expressions. He smells thickly buttered popcorn. The musty smell of the attic fades a little.

Michael wants to go to Hob because he's the only one in this strange new place that Michael knows. But Hob is not who he used to be. Hob has become someone to be avoided.

Michael turns around, walks in the opposite direction, faces blurring by.

Then a very white face breaks through the crowd. A head bobbing above the others. A clown. His eyes lock to Michael's as they near each other. The clown stops. Behind him, on a big building across the way, Michael sees a wooden sign, burned black letters reading:

freekshow:
tonite and every nite

There is no door to the building.

A long arm reaches down for Michael. The crowd seems to fade away to the edges of his vision.

The clown's hand is firm but slightly damp on Michael's shoulder.

"Are you lost, son?" The clown's voice is thick with gravel.

Michael does not answer.

"Son?" The clown's throat is a rock grinder; the words he spits out are hard, round pebbles.

"Yes," Michael says, because he is.

"Fine, then. See that big sign right over there?" The clown leans down, points over his shoulder with his free hand at the

Freekshow sign, and squeezes Michael's shoulder a little more. "That there is where you can get found."

This close to the clown's face, Michael sees all his wrinkles. His makeup is perfect. It's smooth and white, and the colours—the reds, blacks, blues, and oranges—look like real skin. Michael reaches up and touches the clown's face, runs his finger down his cheek. The clown smiles, revealing slick black teeth. They look like stumps of charred wood.

"It doesn't come off," the clown says.

Michael moves his eyes to look at the Freekshow building, ignores the clown's last comment. "How do I get in?"

"Don't have to get in," the clown says. "Just stand in front. Someone will find you. Someone who's supposed to find you will come along, and there you'll be."

A fly buzzes around the clown's head. Two, three flies. He brushes them away, smacks his flabby lips, clears his throat, warming up the grinder. But before he gets to say anything else, another voice cuts in.

Hob.

The clown straightens up, takes his hand from Michael's shoulder, puts his head down under Hob's gaze and walks away, white head bobbing above the crowd once more.

"Found your way in, I see," Hob says, taps his cane. "The third note stirred this up, Mr. Head. You have only yourself to blame this time."

"I haven't even read the third note yet, Hob."

"I told you to be careful, but you didn't listen. And now you're at the carnival. Now you're in the Freekshow, like the rest of us."

"But how was I supposed to know about the note? I couldn't have *not* found it, Hob."

In the middle of Michael's last sentence, Hob took out his pocket watch. Now he's tapping his foot, waiting again.

"Where's Marla, Hob?" Michael feels he needs to speak to throw Hob off of whatever he's doing. Michael needs Hob to think about something else so that he'll pay attention to him.

Hob sighs deeply, looks at Michael like he's an injured dog on the side of the road. "Marla is here, Mr. Head. She's a very big part of the Show, you know. But the Show itself is very big, and you're such a little boy, there's no way you'll find her. No way at all."

He smiles and winks at Michael.

A fat man in striped pyjamas rides by on a unicycle. Someone claps at him.

"What did the clown tell you, Mr. Head? You do know that a clown cannot be trusted, don't you?"

Michael watches as the unicycle man runs into another fat man on a unicycle—this one wearing spotted pyjamas. They fall together in a heap. The one in spotted pyjamas has a bloody lip. The crowd applauds.

"He said that being a clown is loads of fun," Michael says, "and that I should think about being one when I get older."

Hob's bushy eyebrows knit together. "Yes, well . . ." is all he says, because he's not used to Michael lying to him.

"Goodbye, Hob," Michael says, and makes his way over to the Freekshow building.

To Michael's back Hob says, "You won't find her, Mr. Head, and even if you do, you won't know if it's really her."

Michael doesn't turn around, but Hob knows Michael heard him. Michael hears him whistling as he walks away. When Michael figures Hob's back is turned, he looks over his shoulder, and he's talking to the man Michael first saw him with, clapping the guy on the back again, their heads turned toward each other, the both of them smiling like sharks.

Michael notices that the unicycle guys are back up on their bikes and riding around again, weaving between people; the one who split his lip wipes at it occasionally. Old men and boys point and smile at them.

Michael is at the Freekshow sign, standing directly beneath it. Across the dirt street is a man selling small inflatable pigs on sticks. The pigs have Xs for eyes and their tongues hang from their mouths like they've just been strangled. The pigs aren't pink, but dark grey. People are lined up, pushing and shoving to get one.

Looking to his right, Michael sees a tall pole with a dead mime strapped to it. A dirty little boy wanders up to the mime, stands at his feet, staring up. He pokes the mime once in the belly. The mime does not move. The boy giggles and walks across the street to stand in line for a strangled pig.

There is nothing but death and dirt here.

Michael glances up at the single ride at this carnival—the Ferris wheel—and notices that there are no people in the cars. He looks to the base of the ride and sees that there is no operator, either. The wheel is just left to spin and spin on its own.

Five minutes pass. Ten. Michael's feet begin to ache a little. He sits cross-legged in the dirt and watches the dust that people kick up as they walk by settle on his shoes and jeans. He keeps thinking about the Freekshow building, that it must have doors. Every building has a way in and a way out.

"I can take you to her. I know the way," says a voice beside him. Michael looks to his left and there is a pair of legs. He follows the legs up to the torso, up to the head. It is a short man clothed entirely in brown. His face and hands are the same colour as his clothes. He is walking filth and he is speaking to Michael. "I know the way," the dirty little man repeats, and tilts his head to look down at Michael.

"The way where?" Michael asks.

"I can take you to her," the man says again, and walks into the crowd.

LETTER

MICHAEL IS BACK in the attic, still standing up, staring out the window. It's very dark outside and things are silent in the house. As quietly as possible, Michael pushes the stairs to the hall floor and climbs down. He hears his father snoring in his bedroom. He creeps over to his and Stephen's room. Stephen's in bed, too. Asleep.

No one is bothered that they don't know where Michael is.

Maybe the dead-mothers-and-aunts plot extends to Stephen. Maybe he and the boys' father knew Michael was up in the attic, had a good laugh together, and just left him to visit with mother.

Softly down the stairs, Michael unlocks the front door, pulls it open.

It's one of those nights when a kid can walk out onto his front lawn and feel like he's the only person in the world. Everything is so still. The moon occasionally peeks out from behind puffy black clouds.

There are no such things as dogs anymore—not live ones anyway. Stars do not exist. Cars were never invented.

There's only Michael and the frog in the grass.

At Michael's feet, near the curb, near the garbage can, near the dead dog, near the third letter, is a little brown frog. He blows his little sac out from under his chin. Puffs it out, sucks it in. Puffs it out, sucks it in again. And Michael knows it's a *he*, because all frogs—like all other creatures on earth—are male.

Michael takes the lid off the garbage can quietly.

Frog sucks in.

Michael rips a small hole in the wet garbage bag and pushes his hand down inside. Slick decay. Hollow eye sockets.

Frog puffs out.

Michael feels along the dog's jawline and there's the note. He's careful with his fingers to determine the full size of the note; he doesn't want to just yank on it and tear it in half.

Carefully peeling it off the bone, he hears the frog suck in again. He wonders if this is normal behaviour for a frog out in the suburbs. Maybe suburban frogs act differently than swamp frogs—however it is that swamp frogs act.

Michael pulls his hand from the garbage bag. Frog puffs out.

Then frog puffs out again, and Michael looks down at him. He must have missed something. What happened? Frog didn't suck in.

"You didn't suck in," Michael tells the frog. The frog doesn't acknowledge him, just sucks in and puffs out twice quickly.

Then before he can get the lid on the garbage can again, the frog jumps right in. Michael hears him land against the garbage bag. The frog hops around a couple of times—perhaps getting comfortable—and Michael hears him suck in once more.

The frog is keeping the dog company.

Michael wipes his dirty hands on the grass and walks back to the house, thinking that maybe everything isn't about him. Just maybe things go on around him that have absolutely nothing to do with him at all.

Back inside the house it's all shadows and silence. Groping his way blindly through the dark living room, he wonders if the ink on the note will be too smeared to make out the words.

Through to the kitchen, he grabs a cloth off the counter near the sink, wets it, brings it back into the living room. He sits on the couch and flicks on the nearby light. The lampshade glows a deep red.

The note is folded into quarters. Gently, Michael unfolds it; even more gently, he wipes it clean. His heart flops around inside his ribcage.

Three's the charm, lucky three, he thinks. *This is the one. This is the one where it all comes clear and mom's coming home.*

The words on the page are smudged, the ink badly smeared in places, but he can just make it out:

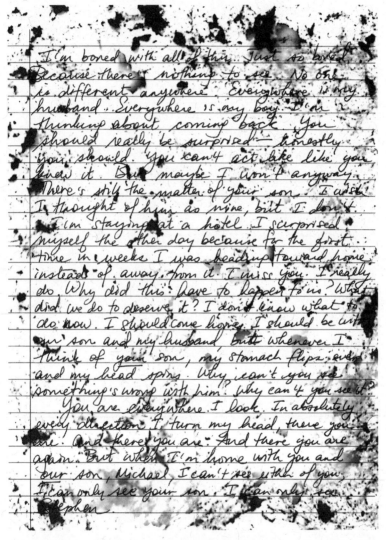

Michael decides right then and there that he is not going to show the note to his brother. Looking down at the damp letter in the red glow, Michael thinks: *What is wrong with him? What is so wrong with him that he made our own mother leave her family?*

There are tears somewhere inside him. Somewhere in and down. But they're not finding their way out tonight. Not when the night is so still and the lamp is glowing so softly and the frog is so happy with his new friend, the dead dog, the messenger who brought him this note, but the tears are pushing up through Michael, welling, coming to the surface, even though his surface isn't the same.

Will never be the same.

Michael folds up the letter, turns off the light, gropes his way through the living room again, through the afterimages of lamplight that dot the walls, the carpet, the staircase.

Upstairs, Michael puts the new letter in a different place than the other two, so Stephen won't find it, then crawls into bed.

He can't hear Stephen breathing below him, and for the first time that he can remember he doesn't climb down the ladder to see if his brother is still alive.

SOMETHING FOR MICHAEL

THE THIRD DEAD dog the Numbers find while digging in the backyard the next day is one dead dog too many, and they decide they'd rather not find a fourth.

The boys' father phones up the company and complains that the crew has left without finishing the job. The Director of Big Yellow Digging Things on the other end of the line tells their father that he'll send out another crew to take over where the first Numbers left off.

When asked, their father says he doesn't know why the crew left.

The new Numbers are all white. After they work for a few hours the boys' father invites them in for coffee, tea, Coke, spring water, donuts, muffins, anything he has in the cupboards. He says he'll order out for pizza come suppertime. They all thank him over and again. He says it's nothing.

It's nothing.

Stephen and Michael are in their room. Stephen's reading the new *Incredible Hulk* comic book. Michael's thinking about the third letter, hoping his brother won't ask about it.

Stephen somehow snatches the thought out of Michael's head and, without looking up from a panel where The Hulk is smashing a shed to tiny splinters, says, "You've read the third letter, Mikey. What did it say?"

Michael dangles his feet over the side of his bunk, looks down at the top of Stephen's head. He tries to bore into his brother's skull, snatch Stephen's thoughts like he just did Michael's. But when he tries, he gets nothing.

Michael thinks Stephen can do anything. He is as much a comic-book hero as Spider-Man or Batman or any of the other superheroes in his collection.

And now Michael has to lie again. So even though Michael knows Stephen will know he's lying, he goes on with the lie. He blurts it out and just waits for Stephen to call him on it. "I didn't find the third letter, Stephen."

Stephen turns the page. In the panel Michael sees around Stephen's head, The Hulk is picking up some guy and lifting him over his head. The Hulk's teeth are very white. He's snarling. The man above him is screaming.

"Sure you did, Mikey. What did it say?"

"Why don't you tell me, since you seem to know everything anyway?"

Stephen stands up, walks over to Michael's dresser where he knows he put the first two letters. He opens the little brown box that contains some hockey cards, one Canadian quarter, and the first two letters from their mother.

"Where'd you put it?" Stephen asks. As usual, he won't look at Michael.

"I told you, I didn't find it."

"Yes, that's what you told me," Stephen says.

Michael remembers what the letter said, and how much of an advantage he would have over his brother if Stephen knew their mother loved Michael most.

"It's okay, Mikey," Stephen says, sitting back on his bunk beneath Michael, picking up *The Incredible Hulk* comic again. "You don't have to tell me what the letter said"—and this is where their mother comes between them; this is the start of it, right here—"But I know you found it," he continues, "and I know it's in this room somewhere. I'll look for it when you're gone and I'll find it. Because I deserve to know what it says, just as much as you do."

What Stephen says hurts Michael more than anything he's ever said or done to him before. Michael knows Stephen doesn't love him like a brother should, but the calm they had between them is coming apart. It's Michael's lies that are causing it, and he knows that. Stephen knows it, too—he's pulling further away, getting even colder toward Michael than he already was. But even knowing all this, Michael can't say anything to make it better. All he can do is admit his guilt to try to make it easier on himself.

"I know you deserve to know, Stephen, but I can't tell you. I know you'll find the letter, but you won't find it with any help from me."

Stephen flips the page in his comic book. Flips another one. Then another. It's the last page of the issue, and the final frame shows a close-up of The Hulk's angry face.

"These new guys won't find any more dogs," Stephen says. "You know why, Mikey?"

"No," Michael says, quietly. "Why?"

"'Cause the guy who buries them in the yard came last night and dug the remaining ones out and took them back. I saw him do it."

Michael doesn't know what to say to this, so he says nothing.

"I bet you want to see him, though, don't ya, Mikey? Well, I think he's coming back tonight. Do you want to see him? I can show you. We can watch him together, Mikey. You'll have to stay up a little bit longer than you usually do—" and out from under his bunk come his sticks, clatter-clack "—but it'll be worth it, Mikey. Honestly, it will."

"Okay, Stephen, we'll wait up for him together tonight. Do we just stand at the window and watch?"

"Yeah, but we have to turn out the lights or he'll see us."

Watching Stephen fiddle with his sticks from above is hypnotizing. Michael sees patterns form in the way his

75

brother's hands move, the sounds the sticks make. They're clearer than before. Michael had always sensed a kind of pattern, but now, seeing them from the same angle Stephen sees them, it's sort of like a language. One that Michael can't understand, but one that he thinks he could learn.

"What do you think he'll bring tonight, Stephen?" Michael says, and things feel sort of normal again. There is no real caring in the way they speak—Michael has grown used to that—but at least that feeling of familiar comfort is back.

But then Stephen says this thing—and he's forever doing this, and Michael doesn't think it will ever stop—this thing he says unbalances them again. He says, "I think he's going to bring something for you tonight."

By the end of the day, the new Numbers finish digging the hole. They're coming back tomorrow to build the actual pool. The boys' father is excited, he tells his sons, because he's really looking forward to swimming again in his own backyard. He misses it, he says.

Michael and his father share a cup of coffee in the kitchen, watching the new Numbers sweat under the sun. Michael and his father never speak when they're sharing coffee; they just take turns sipping from the mug. Michael likes to think this brings them closer than any words possibly could. Bits of blue pool panels glint and flash Michael in the eyes now and again, reminding him of the car hood, the weed killer, the trip to the hospital. It seems such a long time ago.

His father hasn't even brought up the dead dogs. Wouldn't a normal father have mentioned it? Wouldn't a normal father have asked his sons if they had any idea how three dead dogs wound up buried in his backyard? Michael doesn't know much about other people's fathers, but he has listened to them on the radio, seen them in Stephen's ridiculous comic books, and any of them would probably have asked their sons about the dead dogs.

Flies crash themselves into the sun-heated glass of the sliding kitchen door. Certainly more tales of terror about the boys' father have circulated in Fly World and these poor souls are trying desperately to get out of the house.

When the coffee is gone, Michael's father gets up from his chair and heads to the couch for a midday nap—an open challenge to all flies with the nerve to take on a legend. He tells Michael to wake him up if the Numbers need anything.

Left alone, sitting in the kitchen, Michael thinks about tonight. He's excited. Something for him, Stephen said. Digging Guy was going to bring something for Michael.

Maybe it would be something Michael could bring with him to the carnival. Maybe something he could give to Marla to show her how much he misses her.

DIGGING GUY

AS NIGHT GETS closer, Michael's not sure whether he wants to meet Digging Guy tonight or go back to the carnival and follow the dirty little man to wherever it is he thinks he can take him.

There is a small rocking chair—really much too tiny for Stephen or Michael to sit in comfortably—near their bedroom window. Michael sits in this chair, all scrunched down in it, and stares out at the giant hole in the backyard.

Shadows from the tall trees in the yard lengthen and fall into the hole. The flip of Stephen's comic book pages coming from his bunk make Michael tired and he feels himself getting sleepy.

He wonders if this window could take him to the carnival, too, if he let it.

His eyelids get so heavy, he dozes off. He wakes up suddenly to find Stephen standing very still right beside him. "Shh," Stephen whispers. "He'll be here soon. You don't want to scare him away. I'll turn off the light."

He walks across the room, snaps off the overhead light, returns to his position beside Michael. Michael leans forward, squinting, wiping sleep out of his eyes. He feels strange, disconnected in the way you do when you fall asleep during the day and wake up again when the sun has gone down.

A few minutes pass in complete silence. Michael glances at the alarm clock on Stephen's dresser: 11:14 PM.

"When does he usually come, Stephen?" Michael whispers, not taking his eyes off the yard, scanning back and forth, eyes peeled for movement of any kind.

"Usually between eleven and eleven-thirty. Now be quiet

and just watch, doofus," Stephen whispers back.

Eleven-twenty rolls around. Nothing.

Eleven-twenty-five.

Eleven-thirty. Just the wind, some rustling leaves, and Stephen's breathing in Michael's ear.

Michael keeps his mouth shut until eleven-forty. "So where is he, Stephen?"

Michael looks up at his brother and sees it in his eyes, plain as day. Stephen is smirking a little, and he says, "I guess he's not coming tonight, Mikey. Sorry."

And that's it. He walks to his bunk bed, slides under the covers, rolls onto his side, and turns away from Michael.

Michael has no one to blame for this but himself. He knows that from this point forward neither of them can ever trust the other with anything. No going back. Another sliver of their splintered relationship slides under his fingernails, and he feels like throwing up.

Turning back to the window, he sees someone very clearly reflected in it. Someone standing directly behind him. It's not Stephen. It's not his father.

Michael turns around. The man standing there is holding something in his right hand by his side. A small, flat envelope. He takes a step forward and Michael sees that it's the dirty little man from the carnival.

"My brother . . ." Michael says, unsure of what words are going to come next from his lips, ". . . said you had something for me. I thought you were going to bury it in the backyard."

Stephen does not move. Michael's supposed to think he's asleep, but there's so much between them now that he thinks he might be listening and just choosing not to react.

"The dogs were dead, Michael, and fit to be buried," the little man says. "They worked well enough for what I needed them to do, but now there's no time. You have to follow me back to the carnival. I know where she is. I can take you to her."

Michael notices that the dirty little man's voice is not as dirty as the rest of him. His clothes are brown and filthy, and his skin is nearly black with what looks like caked-on mud and ash. But his voice is pure, clear, ringing.

Michael is annoyed that Stephen knew about the dirty little man—only Stephen knew him as the Digging Guy. Michael's annoyed because he and his brother's worlds aren't supposed to overlap like this. It isn't fair at all.

"Don't you want to see her again, Michael? Don't you want to know the answers to all this?" The little man holds out the tiny envelope. "There's another letter in here from your mother," he says. "Come on up to the attic with me. Through the window. There's not a lot of time."

Suddenly, Michael feels Marla near him, feels her hand in his, smells her hair, sees her dress. He closes his eyes and the feelings grow stronger in his mind.

With his eyes still closed, he gets out of the rocking chair and follows the dirty little man out of his room, up the stairs to the attic, and through the window. He doesn't open his eyes at all. He doesn't have to.

Marla leads the way.

TURKEY-THING

THE DIRTY LITTLE man's head gets swallowed by the crowd. Michael feels the ghost of Marla's hand fall away from his as he follows him. Michael keeps walking, hoping to catch a glimpse of the dirty little man, a stinking sea of weirdness parting before him.

Men dragging animals behind them on thick, fraying ropes: pigs, dogs, cats, sheep, raccoons, other animals Michael doesn't know the names of. Some dead, some not. When the weight becomes too much for the man pulling the animal, he motions with his hand frantically for his son—or any nearby boy—to push the beast, or pick it up and help carry it. Where they're going with these creatures, Michael has no idea.

Between these scenes of struggle are other men hugging tightly wrapped pink or blue bundles close to their chests. Once in a while, they tuck in their chins and speak to the bundles, smiling warmly.

Michael watches one man as he passes close by on his left side. The man's smile stretches clear across his face, brown-and-yellow-stained teeth leering down at whatever's inside his blue bundle. A grubby finger pokes around inside the blanket he supports with his free arm as he tickles and coos. He trips over the tip of a rock sticking out of the ground, stumbles, almost rights himself, and then pitches forward into the dirt, the bundle coming unravelled, sprawling its contents under the steady stream of filthy shoes coming in the opposite direction. These shoes slide and twist, their owners nearly tripping and falling themselves.

Painted rocks. Big one for a head; two smaller ones to make up the torso and lower body.

No one stops to help this man pick up his rocks and wrap them back up in his bundle. The blue cloth collects dusty footprints; the man bursts into tears, brings his hands up and covers his face. He pulls himself to his feet, anger suddenly bubbling from his lips, spitting sharp words into the air. His rocks and cloth forgotten, he stumbles through the crowd until he finds the free end of a rope attached to a dead goat. The goat's belly is bloated with flies and maggots. The crying man takes up the rope in one of his dirt-encrusted hands, slings it over his shoulder, and trudges through the streets with the other men. The goat's middle opens up wide as it's dragged over the rough dirt road.

Michael looks up and down the street at ground level and notices patches of pink, patches of blue peeking out from under the dust. Rocks like the ones from the crying man's bundle litter the street on both sides, being tripped over, kicked around, picked up, examined, dropped again. Some are pushed under the wooden porches of buildings; most are just forgotten.

Michael hears a low rumbling and is forced to quickly step out of the way of two astonishingly fat men rolling their way through the crowd like bowling balls. They've been tipped on their sides and are being pushed through the streets by even larger men. When the bowling ball men lose steam, the giant bowlers behind are there to heave them on their way. Michael steps out of the path of one of these balls, only to watch as a young boy, maybe six years old, gets steamrollered by this beast. Small bones crunch; the boy cries in agony. The human bowling balls roll on. And as with the roped animals, Michael doesn't know where this parade of massive human flesh is going.

The little boy is screaming, writhing in the middle of the road with his broken legs and twisted back. Screaming but not asking for help, because he knows no one is listening.

Michael knows on some level that these men are already

dead. They've created legends and myths out of themselves, out of their lost women—if women ever existed. They created gods where none used to be, created markers and signposts of their decay, their jealousy for powers they didn't and would never have. And then followed them. Death in the Belly. Painted rocks to replace babies.

These thoughts are mice scrambling around inside Michael's head looking for cheese, but looking harder for mousetraps.

Pushing past more filthy people, pigs on sticks, black balloons, Michael spots the dirty little man again, up ahead, moving quicker; he's almost lost him. Then the man slows, turns to his right, heads toward a dark purple tent, and slips inside. There is a giant eyeball painted on the closed flap of the tent. Almond-shaped, with long eyelashes. Michael brushes the flap aside and steps through.

He hears someone shuffling cards. A smoky overhead light swims out of the blackness. Underneath it is a card table. Four men sit around the table, laughing, puffing on pipes and cigarettes. They all wear overalls and long beards. Michael sees right away that one of them is hiding cards in his beard, but no one else seems to notice.

Michael doesn't see the dirty little man in the tent.

As Michael walks closer, he sees in the middle of the table, on a bed of unlit cigarettes, what looks like a turkey. But it's not. It's a small sack of grain, sort of shaped like a turkey, with one wet, glassy eye swivelling about in what would be its head if it had a proper one. The eye tracks Michael as he comes closer. The grain inside the bag shifts a little as if the turkey-thing is trying to position itself for a better look at him.

Michael stops near the edge of the table, waiting for someone to notice him. No one does. Except for the turkey-thing, which won't take its eye off him for a second.

Michael says to the turkey-thing, "Quit looking at me

like that. I'm the only one out of you all that isn't filthy and disgusting."

The turkey-thing looks like its trying desperately to blink, but it can't. Michael doesn't think it has an eyelid. Instead, a sticky fluid dribbles from the bottom of its eye, gets absorbed into the grain sack. Maybe Michael's wrong, though—maybe he's hurt its weird little feelings and it's crying.

The man to the left of the guy with the cards stuffed into his beard suddenly whoops loudly. "Hooey! Full house, you old bastards!" he yells, lays his cards down in front of him, and stomps his foot in the dirt beneath the table. When his knee comes back up, it knocks against the table and the turkey-thing flops around a bit.

"Settle down, now, Horace," says another guy, this one with his back to Michael. "Ya don't wanna rattle Big Jimmy outta his coma, do ya?"

The card players look toward the guy with the cards in his beard. Big Jimmy sits silently, scratches his beard, and very obviously removes one of the cards there, puts it in with the rest of his hand. Big Jimmy lays his cards softly down on the table, looks around at the other men. He looks like he wants to ask a question, but his mouth doesn't move; he just keeps looking from man to man to man and back again.

"Four of a kind. Son of a bitch," says Horace. The remaining card in Jimmy's beard flutters to the table.

"'Nother hand, boys?" asks Horace.

The man on Jimmy's right curses under his breath, shakes his head, looks around the table, then over toward where Michael's standing. He stares at Michael hard while Horace shuffles the cards and deals.

"So go on and take it, son. Take the sack."

For a moment, Michael can't say anything. Then: "You can see me?"

"'Course I can see ya. Now go on and take that sack along outta here so's we can get back to our game."

"The sack?" Michael asks. The turkey-thing appears to be sweating now.

"Yeah, the sack, the sack, take the damn sack and run along, son. Ya want my help or not?" The man turns back to the card game.

Michael looks at the turkey-thing. It's fidgeting a lot now and the eye in its head is swivelling harder, flopping back and forth so much that eye juices slosh over its rim, sinking into the grain sack.

Michael takes a few more steps, reaches into the middle of the table, and snatches the sack. He tips it upside down as he pulls it away from the pile of cigarettes. Eye goo drips a dotted line to the edge of the table. A couple of cigarettes come unstuck from its back and fall to the floor. No one raises his eyes to look at Michael. Big Jimmy threads more cards into his beard.

Michael stuffs the turkey-thing under his arm and backs out of the tent, lifting the flap with his free hand.

Out on the street, unsure of where to go or what to do next, Michael wonders where the dirty little man went, and how he's going to find Marla.

He looks down at the turkey-thing. Its grains squirm around inside its sack, and slowly its eye rolls upward. Michael follows its gaze. It's looking ahead, straight down the road, farther into the carnival.

Michael starts walking, kicking small clouds of dust in front of him, stopping only to buy a strangled-pig balloon at a nearby stand. The little strangled pig with Xs for eyes bobs around at the end of its stick in the hot breeze. It's laughing at him. Dark red tongue waggling.

Michael follows the turkey-thing's eye through the streets of the carnival. He wonders if it will understand him if he talks to it. He wants to ask it if it's leading him to Marla, if it knows that's who he's here to find.

Its eye leads him past more men dragging things behind them—this time it's dead horses. Two men to a horse, puffing and panting, red-faced.

Turning down another street, Michael thinks he sees a woman walking through the crowd of men, but as he gets closer, he sees that it's just a man wearing a mask with makeup on it and a too-tight dress. Michael watches the man walk past him, tripping in his high heels once in a while. A few more of these men walk by, mixed in with the crowd, and Michael notices that they're identical in face and dress. They're like cheap Halloween costumes, pulled straight from the racks of department stores. None of these men-women are pulling dead horses.

A few more turns down different streets and Michael's confused. He can't remember which way they've come. And he thinks, too, about the fact that he's thinking "we" when talking about himself and the bizarre turkey-thing under his arm.

He's tired of calling the turkey-thing "the turkey-thing," so he decides he should name it. He stops in the middle of a deserted street—the dead horses and assorted men having abruptly thinned out when he turned the last corner—and thinks about what to call his turkey-thing. He looks down at it as it squirms against his ribcage.

"What should I call you?" he asks it.

It just rolls its eye in the next direction it wants him to walk. He asks it again. Just more rolling.

"Okay," Michael says, "Smithy's your name. Smithy's a tough name and you're a tough turkey-thing."

Smithy twitches a little, then just rolls his eye up again.

"Alright, I'm going," Michael says, and keeps walking. The strangled pig deserves a name, too, Michael supposes, but not yet. Plenty of time for naming pigs.

A few streets behind him, Michael still faintly hears the main part of the carnival. It sounds warped, twisted out of tune. The notes from the music of the Ferris wheel are stretched and overlapping themselves. The sound of wind blowing down this street seems to be trying to straighten the music out, bend it back into shape, but it's not working. People's laughter sounds like barrels turned on their sides and rolled down wooden stairs; little boys' screams reach Michael's ears—abandoned teakettles, whistling away to no one; the bits of speech he hears between the buildings are dry leaves crunching under dirty feet.

Passing one more intersection of streets, looking left and right, he sees no one. There's just the wind and the far-away noises from the carnival. But even those get quieter as he crosses the street.

Driven into the dirt on the other side of the road is a signpost—the only one Michael has seen. A large square of wood has been nailed to the top of the post; burned into this square is the following:

THIS IS THE END OF THE CARNIVAL.
NO MORE STREETS THIS WAY.
TURN BACK.
GO ENJOY THE CARNIVAL.
THE CARNIVAL IS WHAT YOU ARE HERE FOR.
The Management, Freekshow Inc.

Michael looks at Smithy. Smithy rolls his eye up the street. The grains inside him shiver and roll around so that Michael feels like Smithy's trying to kick him.

Michael looks past the sign, takes a few more steps, and sees that a building tucked alongside a brick wall cuts the road off completely. A few more steps to the left and he sees a door. The door is wide open. He can't see what's inside from here, but Smithy kicks him harder and eye goo drips down his sack.

Three steps lead up to the doorway. As he approaches the building and climbs them, he sees a child's drawing of a dead mime strapped to a post to the right of the door. The mime has no eyes—only a white face, a green nose, and black lips—and its head is lumpy and hangs to one side, as if its neck were broken. Where its belly is are the scribbled words "poke here."

A dirty little boy steps out of the darkness of the doorway and pokes Michael softly in the belly.

He suddenly wakes up in his attic. He's lying on the cold floor with no Smithy, no strangled pig, and the rumble of machinery and the shouts of the Numbers in his ears.

BACK DOOR

THOUGH HIS FATHER and Stephen know Michael was up in the attic all night, neither of them says a word about it at breakfast. Stephen clatters his knife and fork together once in a while—the boys' father won't let Stephen bring his sticks to the table—and something like understanding passes between them. Michael suspects his father has learned Stephen's stick language, so now they can talk about him while he's sitting right in front of them.

But that's okay, because neither of them understands Smithy's grain-shifting language and, even though Michael doesn't either, he will. He'll learn it, and he and Smithy can talk about all sorts of things. Then Stephen, Michael, and their father will be even again.

Later that day, Michael watches from his bunk as the Numbers finish building the pool. Tomorrow they'll fill it with water, and then the boys' father will make a weekend event of the Official First Swim in the New Pool. And by the weekend, Michael thinks he'll be dead, so he figures he'd better find Marla before then. Wherever he goes after his father kills him, he thinks, he's sure he'll be with Marla, if he can find her.

Michael wonders how he'll get to the carnival tonight. Will it be through sleep? Through the window in the attic? Or maybe some new way? Like maybe if he concentrates hard enough, he can make himself go there whenever he wants to. Because thoughts are powerful. Thoughts and ideas change people, change the world.

Falling asleep that night, Michael doesn't feel Marla's hand in his. He just feels nervous. He knows that soon he's going to have to see Hob again. And he doesn't think Smithy or the strangled pig are any sort of protection at all. He knows they're both cowards and that they'll abandon him in a second when Hob finally comes around. He needs to find someone reliable.

As the sounds of the road outside the window fade away, Michael feels, like through a thin pillow, the little boy poking him in the belly again. Smithy's under his arm now, and the balloon pig's in his other hand. He looks down, looks over to the painted mime on the wall. He pushes the boy to the side, in front of the mime, and the boy's finger continues poking the air. He turns himself around and keeps his finger going, now poking the mime's belly.

Michael turns to the right and there's another little boy, peeking around the corner of the building. Michael wonders where they're all coming from.

"Go in, mister," this second boy whispers. "Go on in. You found the back door. No one finds the back door to the Freekshow unless they're supposed to."

The two boys look like brothers. Michael looks at the one poking the mime.

"Oh, and don't worry about him," says the other boy, nodding his head in the direction of the belly-poker. "He'll stop pretty soon. Hob comes around every once in a while to wash the mimes off the buildings. He only wants us poking real mimes. Real people. You know how he is."

Yes, Michael knows how Hob is. Great and Terrible.

"I'd leave the pig behind, though, mister. You don't want two voices telling you what to do. Just makes any decision you might have to make in there that much harder."

Michael wants to ask why he should leave the pig behind and not Smithy, but he knows better. Small boys at carnivals know the rules. They know the rules of all the games, all the rides, all the relationships. They make it their business. But the boy answers Michael anyway:

"You named him, so you can trust him," the boy says. "And who knows? Maybe Smithy's counting on you a little bit, too, you know?"

The little boy smiles and disappears around the side of the building again. The boy poking the drawing of the mime suddenly stops. He lowers his hand and looks up at Michael, reaches a hand up and gently pulls the strangled-pig balloon from Michael's fingers. He follows the other little boy around the side of the building, and Michael's left staring at the eyeless mime.

For the first time, he's actually a little bit scared.

Smithy struggles under his arm, signalling that Michael should carry on. Smithy's eye is pointed straight into the darkness of the Freekshow building. Michael follows it in.

Then he's stepping down a set of wooden stairs, because everything here is made of wood. Or some darker cousin of it. Smithy's eye sparkles in the dying light coming from behind and above them. Darker and quieter until they reach a landing. Poking his toe out over the edge of the landing, Michael feels the next step. The light above fades and fades until it's just a heavy yellow haze at his back. He carries on down the steps until he comes to another flat section of floor. This time he doesn't feel like he's on a landing. This feels bigger, wider.

It's colder down here. Michael shivers a little; Smithy's eye seems crisper, less gooey. Smithy struggles against Michael's ribs and swivels his watery eye toward Michael. Michael wishes now that he hadn't listened to that little boy outside; he wishes he still had his strangled-pig balloon, so he would have some excuse to just turn around and walk back up those stairs. Wouldn't have Smithy's terrible, wet eye driving him onward.

But he doesn't, so he's walking again. He has walked a lot lately. Everything he needs seems to be so far away.

Michael passes through a doorway and he's somehow back

in the tent with the old men playing cards. The overhead light is the same; the smoke hovering beneath it is the same; but the men playing cards are not. The men are just shadows of themselves, smoke drifting right through them, and Michael sees that the fourth player—the one who told Michael to pick up Smithy and move along—is not a man anymore. It is a woman.

It is Marla.

His Marla. There she is, playing shadow cards with shadow men. Michael's choking on a lump, but, like with his father and Stephen, he can't cry in front of these men, even if they are just shadows.

Marla looks exactly how Marla looks. Her sundress, her green eyes, her soft, soft hands. Flesh and bone among shadows. The black shapes of the men motion to each other how men do when playing cards.

Marla turns her head toward Michael and says, "Mr. Head. Put Smithy back on the table now." She is smiling, but her voice is hard. "You don't need him anymore."

Hob's words come back to Michael, and he doesn't know what to do. Hob said that even if he does find Marla, he wouldn't know that it was really her. So how can he trust her? Why did Hob have to go and say that? Michael shouldn't doubt his Marla. She loves him, and he loves her, and she's the only one who doesn't try to fill him up with herself. The only one who doesn't try to assemble herself inside Michael's head piece by piece. She doesn't want to create a mirror image of herself like everyone else does. She's different, and she's his, and he can't let Hob spoil her, he can't let Hob's lies wreck who she is, so Michael steps closer to the table, and no way he can look at Smithy right now, because he knows what his eye is doing, it's staring right at Michael, and he knows if he looks, he'll finally understand the grain-language and the shifts and squirms will all make sense and Smithy will try to tell Michael not to put him back on the table, but he has to, he can't let Hob win, and he's only a couple of steps away now, and there's Marla's smiling face and her wonderful smell, and on the table, in place of the bed of cigarettes that he took Smithy from is now a bed of letters, letters from his mother, and Marla's just waiting, breathing in smoke and waiting, and then Smithy's out from under Michael's arm, he's kicking and squirming but Michael's not looking, although he's crying, and that's also why he's not looking, because Smithy helped him, Smithy showed him the way, and now he's betraying him right here, in this smoky Freekshow full of shadowy men, and there he is now—

Lying on the letters. But he's not kicking anymore.

The grains in his sack aren't moving at all.

Marla is still smiling, but Michael's gulping in air because Smithy's eye isn't moving, and Michael's nose is running, and he's wiping his eyes, and everything is shimmering, and the dirty little man from the carnival—

Swims out of the dark behind the card table and walks right by. For just a moment, it looks like he has a beard, but Michael blinks tears away and it's gone.

Michael, snot dribbling from his top lip, turns around and watches him go. The dirty little man walks out through the doorway, and speaks as he mounts the steps that lead back outside: "I can take you back." His voice sounds thinner than before. Thin and sad. "I know the way."

Michael looks back to Marla.

A shadow card flutters from Big Jimmy's beard, lands softly on the table.

Marla is still smiling, but all of her attention is now on Smithy.

"When will I see you again?" Michael asks Marla. He

wipes his face with his arm, and it's getting colder now; he can see his breath.

Marla doesn't answer.

This isn't Marla. This isn't his Marla, Michael thinks.

She turns to Michael, then, and says, "I *am* your Marla, Mr. Head. But you have to go now. Follow the dirty little man back home. Hob knows. Hob knows about all of this. This is his place, his carnival. But playing the game his way, on his terms, in his world, is the only way it will work."

"The letters . . ." Michael says, looking over at them on the table.

"Smithy has released the letters—now you'll find more. And you'll see me again. You will. I'll make sure Hob doesn't follow you out of here. Now go."

"Hob? Hob's here?"

"In the lower levels, Mr. Head. You haven't seen them yet, and Hob would like nothing more than to keep you from them, so you *have to go now.*"

Michael starts crying again. Marla's voice isn't made to grind words out of her mouth like this. Michael takes another look at Smithy, unmoving on the table, then turns around and walks toward the stairs. The air gets warmer as he climbs, and then he's up and out of the Freekshow.

The dirty little man stands in the middle of the street—his filthy skin, grubby clothes, and crystal voice fading in Michael's mind; he says, "I know the way."

UNCLE

BREAKFAST AGAIN. MICHAEL heading downstairs to the table. And the boys' father and Stephen chat with their utensils.

Fine day, wouldn't you agree, father? clatters Stephen.

Just so! says their father, and scrapes the back then the front of his knife onto his fork, pretending to be just smearing some egg and beans.

Have I told you that Michael knows about the pool plan?

Oh, he does, does he? their father clinks. *Well, that's just fine, because it isn't like he can do anything about it.* He grins, shovels a forkful of beans into his mouth.

They talk like this a while longer, then their father clears away the dishes, and Stephen slips out the back door to watch the Numbers fill the pool. Water splashes outside. White Numbers crawl around in their black shadows, tidying up, running hose here and there, wiping sweat from their brows. No more dogs have been found, just like the dirty little man said.

But Michael suddenly feels that something is wrong, something has changed—he feels it in the pit of his stomach, like something has been ripped from him, torn away.

There's only one telephone in their house; it's in the kitchen, hanging on the wall. Their father is washing dishes, not paying attention to Michael, but Michael is sure he'll know who he's calling as soon as he picks up the phone. Michael doesn't have friends, so he'll know it's got to be the boys' uncle. To Michael, his uncle is the only other person who actually exists outside of this house. Even the Numbers are just extensions of his father and the things he believes.

Michael gets up from his chair as quietly as possible, walks to the phone, picks up the receiver. Michael's father turns and looks at him. He doesn't say anything, but Michael knows he's going to watch him dial. Stephen, outside staring at the water rumbling into the pool, breaks his gaze, turns his head in Michael's direction, and stares at him through the glass door.

They're waiting.

They're waiting because they know.

Michael's fingers feel like thick blocks of ice as he stabs the number into the base of the phone. The line just rings and rings.

When Michael hangs up and looks back to his father and Stephen, neither of them will meet his eyes.

STEALING FLIES

MICHAEL THINKS HIS father is the Keeper of the Flies. And Stephen, even though Michael's sure he has no idea of it, is just another one of their father's flies.

The only things now that connect Stephen and Michael are the letters from their mother. And even though that's their connection, Michael knows when he finds the next one, as with the third one, he'll have to hide it from Stephen. So even that isn't something they can share anymore.

Tomorrow is Sunday and the pool will be done. Tonight will be Michael's last night to find Marla. If he dies without finding her, he thinks he will be alone wherever he goes. He has been given the chance the find someone who loves him properly—something hardly anyone gets a real chance at—so he has to concentrate really, really hard when he goes in tonight.

Through his confusion, the one thing he still sees clearly is that Marla makes him more into the real him the longer he spends time with her. She sucks out whatever people have stuffed inside him. He can't feel her doing it, but when he's around those people who dig into him, he sees in them the things Marla has taken out. He needs her to do this more; he needs her to suck it all out.

Up in Michael and Stephen's room, Michael takes out the two letters, and tucked beneath them is the third. Stephen obviously found it and put it with the others, so now he knows what it says. How would a boy feel knowing—knowing *for sure*—that he was the reason his mother left his family?

Rereading the letters, Michael hopes there's some hint of where the fourth one might be. Michael feels he needs to find it before Stephen. But people don't write hints about their next letter. That's silly. Michael's hoping for ridiculous things.

Michael's about to cry again, and he feels so foolish. No matter what he thinks he can do to bring Marla nearer, he feels the flies working against him. The tears are nearer because Michael doesn't know what to do, doesn't know where to look, and he has no one to turn to. He's not supposed to feel like this. He's supposed to be detached, far away, content to buzz along as one of his father's flies.

MARLA WAS HERE is what Michael wants to write. He wants to burn it into his skin like the burned letters on the wooden signs at the carnival. Even better would be to burn MARLA *IS* HERE. But the flies buzz louder in his ears and he can't think of any way to stop them, except—

—Marla and her hard words at the Freekshow and how she told him he would find more letters, but she didn't say where, and he knows Marla wouldn't lie to him, it's not possible, so he has to believe her because it's all he has left, so he knows he'll find them, and he has to believe Marla, because Marla said—

They have to play the game by Hob's rules now.

Michael stuffs all three letters into one of his jeans' pockets, then closes his eyes, just for a second.

Just for a second.

CHARCOAL

MICHAEL OPENS HIS eyes to see the charcoal ground and his and Marla's bench. Marla's not sitting on it, but Michael is. In front of him is a cardboard cut-out of Hob. He's looking at his pocket watch, his foot in mid-tap.

Frozen. Waiting for something. Waiting for Michael.

Michael feels like punching him. Michael wants to smack his top hat off his head, rip that pocket watch from his hand and scream as loud as he can in his face that it HAS NO HANDS.

But.

But . . .

He can't do that. He has to play the game by Hob's rules. Like his Marla said.

Michael stands up, slowly circles the cut-out. It seems to be rooted, driven into the charcoal. Michael has to pull it out. That's how Hob would have rigged this. He's so obvious. Michael bends his knees, wraps his arms around the cut-out and pulls. Hard.

Nothing. It won't move. A few more tries, but it's like it's been cemented in.

The cut-out's eyes follow Michael as he circles it. Green suit and top hat. It so badly wants to tap its foot, tell Michael how late it is for some appointment, stroke its goatee, waggle its eyebrows, tear more pieces out of Michael, steal more things he loves, make him doubt them, hide them from him. Hide them and make him play its silly games so he might find them again.

The spider. Michael followed the spider to the carnival, but the spider abandoned him and led him to other insects. Falling apart. The plaster cracked and Michael discovered different parts of himself.

Don't disturb the charcoal, Mr. Head, Hob said. *You don't know what's under there and you don't* want *to know*. All very dramatic.

Michael's and Hob's shoes are the same size. Michael walked in Hob's footsteps. Michael's feet are Hob's feet and he's suddenly feeling a little sick now, because nothing—NOTHING—about him is supposed to be like Hob. Hob is a different creature. He's not even real. If their feet are exactly the same, Michael thinks, then maybe he's not real either, not in any world, and maybe Marla's not real, and maybe none of this is real, and then Marla would disappear, her and her candy-striped glasses.

Then, Michael thinks, *I would die.*

He feels like vomiting. He feels like puking his guts at Hob's feet—the whole works, intestines, bladder, kidneys, all of it. He wants it to splash into the charcoal and DISTURB it. Because it must not be DISTURBED, and there's another word Michael should get carved into his skin when he thinks of it, when he has time, when he's not just someone's dumping hole. Michael sits down on the bench, his and Marla's bench, head in hands, wanting to die and throw up and make himself hollow.

Empty.

And Hob's done it—

Without even being here. Without even being *real*, he's done it.

Michael's head swims, and when he opens his eyes and lifts his head he can't see straight. But he can see the blurred lines of the cardboard-nobody that did this to him.

And still, with no hands on his pocket watch, with his stroked goatee and tapping foot, his bent little cane, with nowhere to be except the exact places he's not, the charcoal starts to shift, and Hob's won.

The cardboard Hob tips over backward and stares straight up at the empty grey above Michael. The charcoal swirls in small circles where feet might be. Michael steps onto the swirling sections of charcoal. He is suddenly very, very tired. His eyelids are heavy, and he's sinking.

Slipping beneath the charcoal ground, he feels like he's suffocating. He couldn't open his eyes now if he wanted to. But he prefers to keep them closed anyway. It makes it easier to pretend the emotional pieces dropping off him, scattering on the grey beneath him, aren't his. And if they're not his, he's not picking them up. The less of them he has, the more of the real him there might be at the end of all this. Because he knows he's being selfish. He's a selfish little child looking for his mother, or at least someone to replace her.

But I don't deserve this, he thinks. *I don't deserve any of this.*

BUTTON

CHARCOAL SIFTS DOWN around Michael. Filters through thick air to his feet.

Grey snow. It sprinkles him a few more moments, then stops. He looks up. Above him is a blackened ceiling. Charred. Nearly smooth. Little bits of grey charcoal cling to it—the only indicator of his passing through.

Dim light, slivers of yellow run in double bars alongside him in each close wall. There is not enough room to think properly. Not nearly enough. The ceiling is too close and his thoughts shrink away from it.

He's in a tunnel. He sees a door at the end of it. Like the tiny bars of dim light along the walls, there are similar bars shining on a small, square sign on the door—more black wood, charred to smoothness, with what looks like thick silver lettering on it. But he is too far away to read what it says.

The last of the charcoal settles, and he thinks about those cows again, the ones he saw coming home from his uncle's house. He thinks about their soft eyes. Trusting eyes. They are led through life, but have come to accept it. He thinks cows know that they are cows; and cows know what they need, what they're capable of. They are led just as this tunnel leads him—just as whomever put that little sign up at the far end of this tunnel knows he's going to read it. The problem with this is that he's not a cow, no matter how soft or trusting his eyes are. So when he takes his first step out of the charcoal sprinklings, toward the door and the sign that he has no choice but to read, he refuses to moo.

After a couple of steps, he looks behind him at the

charcoal, but the grey is turning to black as he moves away, blending into the floor.

The sign with the silver lettering is to the left of the door, about halfway down the wall. Michael has seen the image on the sign before; he held it in a different form under his arm. It showed him the way; it was the truth and the light. It led him to the carnival. It died for him. That's why Michael knows that this image of Smithy is a lie. Smithy is dead. And the phone just rings and rings.

Besides, it's too easy, he thinks. *Follow in some footsteps and at the end of a dimly lit corridor you'll find the fourth letter from your dead mother.*

The silver *IV* beneath the non-Smithy is shiny. The button to the right of these shiny letters is tempting. It's black, sunk into the sign, burnt in like the non-Smithy, trying to trick Michael by looking the same as its environment.

But Michael knows that this must be just the first level. Game-makers make the opening level easy so you'll keep playing. He's played games by other people's rules before, so this one's easy: Don't push the button—the door won't open anyway.

Simple as that.

But he's a real thinker. He knows that thoughts change people, change the world. So he thinks about how the tunnel might turn sideways, showing him a different way to the fourth letter. Maybe the shifting of the room knocks a Special Brick loose and the *real* button pops out. Perhaps he pushes that button, the letter rolls out from some nifty dispensing machine, he reads it, and another piece of the puzzle is fitted into place. Or maybe the button releases a Crackerjack box (surprise inside!) and there's the letter, folded into a neat square, waiting to be read, waiting to explain his life to him.

Michael's thinking these things, and his eyes are closed

hard, shut so tight he can't even imagine opening them again. Gears in his skull are turning; he sees the words in the letter blurring out of focus the harder he squints to read them. Sailor Jack le Marin and his dog, Bingo, grin madly, waiting for him to give up, throw in the towel, push the wrong button, blow it all when he's come this far.

But he blocks it out; he feels the room turning sideways; he hears that Special Brick sliding into place, revealing the *right* button, not the non-Smithy one, and there it is, in his head, right in his hand, the paper crisp, the writing visible, and he's reading it, reading the words, creating another angle to view his mother by, shedding another flat, grey slice of light on it all to silence her memory with, and—

His eyes flip open. Wet. Gummy.

And nothing has happened.

Nothing at all has happened.

The silver *IV* is very shiny—more shiny, Michael thinks, than before he closed his eyes. And Smithy is familiar. Smooth, black, and familiar. People have gone down all sorts of bad roads just because things looked familiar, so why should Michael be any different?

He pushes the button.

A DARK WALL of rock shoots up in front of Michael; his stomach slams into his throat as he steps into the near-complete blackness inside. The elevator suddenly lurches. Little round circles with numbers in them light up above his head.

11.

10.

The elevator stops. The smooth rock wall slides up. Opens.

A large room. Brown furniture. Brown drapes. One big bookshelf at the back filled with brown books.

Michael steps off the elevator. The rock wall slides down again.

On the brown couch is a boy. He looks a little like Stephen, only he has no eyes. He looks dead, but his chest is rising and falling, so maybe he's just asleep. Michael walks closer to the boy, reaches out and pokes him in the shoulder. When he pulls his finger back, the boy smiles at him. The smile does not reach his eyes because he has none.

The boy sits up and pats the space beside him on the couch. "Sit," he says. He seems happy that Michael is here. Michael sits beside the boy. He says—and Michael's thankful that his voice doesn't sound like Stephen's—he says, "The fourth letter is on the bookshelf."

Michael turns his head to look at the bookshelf again. It's huge. It stretches up and away, a long, skinny ladder attached to it so you can get books off the highest shelves.

"Where am I?" Michael asks, because this doesn't feel like the carnival or the Freekshow.

"On the bookshelf," the boy says again.

"Okay, I know, the letter's on the bookshelf, but where is *this*?" Michael says. "Where are *we*?"

"The tenth floor of the building," the boy answers. "Are the lights in the elevator not working again?"

"The lights work fine, but where is the building?"

The boy's teeth seem to be getting whiter with every word he says, and very soon Michael finds that he can't look at them anymore. "On the bookshelf," the boy says again.

"The building is on the bookshelf?"

"No, the fourth letter, the letter I understand you're looking for, is on the bookshelf."

"Who told you I was looking for a letter?"

"He said you might come here looking for it. He said, very explicitly, he said, 'If someone comes here looking for that letter, be sure you tell him it's on the bookshelf,' so I'm telling you that's where it is."

"Who's 'he'? And why won't you tell me where this building—"

"Please stop asking me about the building. Please stop. Please." The boy's smile finally slips.

They sit in silence, neither of them smiling, neither of them happy at all, but at least now that the boy's mouth is closed Michael can look at his face again.

"Where are your eyes?" Michael asks. "Did Hob take them away?"

"Don't be silly," the boy says, but he's still not smiling. "We all lose something when we come here, don't we? I lost my eyes. So what? You'll lose something, too, you know. Everyone does."

"Oh, I'm not staying," Michael says. "I'm just looking for someone, then I'll be leaving. Her name is Marla. Have you seen anyone else come through here?"

Michael notices from this angle that when the boy lies

back on the couch again his skin is nearly transparent. Michael wonders if he has any blood in him.

"Did they take your blood, too?" Michael asks.

"I have as much blood as anyone else," the boy says, and his voice has a tiny drop of anger in it. "I have as much of everything as anyone else, except for eyes. People have two more than me, but that doesn't make them any better. Not by a long shot."

He is quiet for a second or two, then: "Do you know who I am?"

Michael gets a quick tingle up his spine when the boy asks that. He can't tell him he looks like his brother. Only his brother is his brother . . . but the mouth is the same, the nose, the hair, the build—just the voice and the eyes are different. Though maybe the eyes aren't different. Maybe if he had them, they'd be the same as Stephen's.

"No, I don't know. I don't know who you are."

Michael waits for the boy to tell him who he is, or to say something else, but he says nothing. His smile comes back, though, as if that's his answer.

Michael glances again at the enormous bookshelf. "So how am I supposed to find the letter in all those books?"

"You're not."

"I'm not what?"

"Supposed to find it." The boy sits back up, turns his eyeless head in Michael's direction. "You just have to pay for it and I'll give it to you."

"Pay for it? With what? I don't have any—"

"A story. All you have to do is sit and listen to a story, then I'll go up the ladder and fetch the letter for you."

More things to feed into me, Michael thinks. *More opinions that aren't mine, more words I don't understand, less of me left over to worry about.*

"I don't like stories," Michael says.

Behind the couch is a large, dark window. Rain patters against it. Little rivers run down. An occasional flash of far-off lightning lights up the room.

"You'll like this one," the boy says. "It's about you. Besides, it's standard payment. Words for words. I thought you knew the rules. He said you knew the rules."

I should be somewhere else, Michael thinks. *Anywhere but here. Marla's not here. I need to find Marla. I'm wasting time.*

The pool. There is water in the pool. When he wakes up, it will be the end of his life. He has to see her before he dies. He has to make sure she comes with—

"Come on, kid, settle down." And it's like there's more than one person inside this boy. He speaks older than he looks. Michael finds that he likes the boy because of this.

"Come on," the boy says again as he stands up, taking Michael's hand, walking him over to the big window. Lightning flashes again—this time very close—and blinds Michael for a few seconds. Spots dance behind his eyelids.

"Look out the window," the boy says. "Look straight out as far as you can."

There is nothing to see. Nothing at all. Just small bursts of light every once in a while. Michael's eyes aren't all the way open because he's afraid another close flash of lightning will blind him again.

"What am I looking for?"

"You're not looking for anything. You just have to wait until you see it. You'll know it when you see it. Take my word for it."

Michael looks out, peering closely. After a minute or so, just when he's about to give up, he sees it, far off in the distance. It's hovering against the black backdrop. A pinprick of light. Pulsing. Speaking.

In a language only Michael understands.

✣ Bright day. Really bright. In memory's eye—

—and in Michael's real eyes, too—

—it's blinding.

Because he's being held up to the sun. Someone has rolled him up into a blanket and is shoving him into the sun. It's all he sees. He's wailing and crying, but whoever is holding him won't let him down. He's going to be scorched, burned alive.

Now he feels the arms pulling back and a giant moon of a face is in front of him, eclipsing the sun. He's blinking and blinking and his eyes are watering, but all he sees are spots.

Michael's home.

In the arms of his mother.

She is rocking him, rocking him gently and shushing him, telling him those things that mothers tell their children: that everything is okay, mommy is here. She's wiping his eyes, and her hands are warm, incredibly warm. Her skin slightly rough from whatever job she must do, unless she doesn't have a job, which is just as possible because Michael doesn't know his mother. He has no idea who she is or what she does, but here she is and she's holding him. Holding him tight and fussing with the blankets like real mothers do.

Somewhere, another baby is crying, and the rumble of a truck is telling it to be quiet. The truck is not as soothing as his mother, but then trucks aren't made to be soothing; trucks are made to carry things from one place to another, to get from point A to point B with the least amount of hassle. But screaming babies are a hassle, and trucks are not patient machines.

Right now, in these arms, Michael feels like he's part of something. He doesn't know if it's a family that he feels part of, but he feels part of something bigger than himself. He has no holes dug in him yet; nothing has been yanked out and replaced with something that isn't his. He is a small thing, new to the world, and he's being baptized in flames.

Michael's mother doesn't know. She doesn't understand that when she holds Michael up in this playful way he opens his eyes. She doesn't understand that he can't help himself.

Michael hears a screen door open and close. Michael's mother walks toward the house. Michael's still crying because he can't see anything but a field of black spots. His mother opens the screen door and walks in the house. The truck is still rumbling, but the other baby has stopped crying. Michael knows the truck is speaking the same language as his mother, but it's harder to understand because it's so low. Plus, there's a buzzing sound inside the words. They fly around the room, past Michael's ears, inside his ears, inside his mind, and—

—and there's the other baby. Michael sees him and he's looking right at Michael. He's staring at him. He wants to be where Michael is.

In his mother's arms.

9

THE LIGHT IS still there, far off, silent, unmoving. Standing completely still in the centre of the window. Michael turns around and the boy who is not his brother is climbing slowly up the long, skinny ladder. His arms and legs move like water. When he's nearly to the top, he turns around, yells down to Michael, "Push me!"

Michael walks to the bottom of the ladder, looks up at the boy wobbling up there so high, as if he will fall any second. "Which way?"

"To the right!" the boy shouts down.

Michael pushes him hard right. The ladder creaks and groans as it slides across. The boy holds onto the sides of the ladder, then one arm shoots out as he finds his spot. The boy fiddles with a book, a fat brown volume. Very old looking, like the pages are about to crumble to dust. He slips a hand inside, pulls out a folded sheet of paper, climbs backward down the ladder.

Then he's beside Michael, breathing heavy and holding the letter out in front of him. "Take it," the boy says.

"What's the light in the window?" Michael asks, arms still at his sides, his hands clenched tightly into balls. Not opening to take the letter.

"What do you think it is?" the boy says. "It might be whatever you want it to be, but it might be something of its own choosing. All I can tell you for sure—and not because he told me to withhold anything from you, but just because it's really all I can tell you—is that it's not a light. At least it's not *just* a light."

No one can just give a straightforward answer in this

place, Michael thinks. *You have to work to understand. If you work hard enough, ask the right questions, and watch and listen very closely, you might learn something.* But Michael is not a patient boy. He has no time to figure all of this out.

Very suddenly, Michael feels the need to do something. He needs to feel the smooth skin where the boy's eyes are supposed to be. Michael reaches a hand out, stretches his fingers toward the boy's face. The boy doesn't move and Michael's close to touching. Close to feeling his skin, this skin that shouldn't be here. Michael's fingers connect and the boy still doesn't move. Michael runs his index finger across the skin and it's smooth, just as he'd thought. Hard underneath. Silk stretched over rock.

"Now there's no mystery," the boy whispers. "And are you any better for it? Has it changed anything?"

Michael drops his eyes, takes his hand back, pulls the folded letter gently from the boy, turns and walks toward the wall where the elevator should be. He turns around once to see the boy spread himself out again on the couch.

Michael gets nearer to the wall and the rock slab shoots up from the floor. He walks in and there's the tiny version of Smithy, his friend, sunk in black on the wall. The shiny silver *IV* is gone—in its place is a second button. This new button has a small Up arrow glowing dimly on it. The button beside it now has a glowing Down arrow.

Michael has a choice.

He can't cry like a baby now, even if he wants to, because he has a choice. He can do what he likes. He can go back up, maybe out of here, back home to his father and Stephen and their army of flies. Or he can go down, find Marla. Be with his Marla. Maybe forever.

I will take control of this, he thinks. *I am making this decision. No one else.* He pushes the Down button. The wall slides down, slots into place.

10.

9.

Michael looks out onto the ninth floor. Or what should be the ninth floor, but it's not, because it's just a window. It runs from top to bottom of the elevator, and looks out onto nothing. Just rain and lightning and sky.

And the same pulsing thing from the tenth floor library, far off in the night. Only it's closer on this floor, and it's moving closer still. It has edges now, and doesn't seem nearly as bright as before. Michael catches a hint of a shape whenever the lightning stops. It starts to speak again, and Michael can't do anything to stop listening, because it's in that language made just for him. Rhythmic. Primal. Michael's eyelids are giant flaps of metal pinned to his face and he can't fight it anymore. He can't fight it, so he just—

—lets it come inside. Lets it wash through him. Lets it tell him things he's forgotten.

Like right now, where he's looking. He's looking at his mother. She's watching her boys. Watching them through the screen door at the back of the house as they play in the sand, their father sitting in a ratty lawn chair, reading the newspaper, keeping an eye on the boys. Or pretending to, anyway. Both his eyes are on his newspaper and his head is somewhere with the flies. Maybe up in the attic. Maybe thinking with them, plotting something, in some hole in one of the bricks in the house. Flies love holes and so does their father. He loves to dig them, fill them in with thoughts, pools, whatever he has handy.

But their mother's watching them, and she's smiling. She's smiling because her boys are playing in a sandbox, and it's so perfect because they're having fun together. Michael has a bucket in one of his little hands. He's shovelling sand into it, shovelling, shovelling, and there's Stephen, right beside Michael with his own bucket and doing just like Michael. He looks happy. His smile is like Michael's smile. They look so alike at this age. Nearly twins.

Stephen's bucket almost filled, he scoops sand a bit farther away from himself, near Michael's area of the sandbox, to get the good sand—the top stuff, not the wet, clumpy stuff underneath—and Michael smacks him on the hand with his shovel.

This isn't right. Michael doesn't remember doing this.

Stephen flinches back and holds his hurt hand with his good one, dropping his shovel and bucket in the sand.

"Mine," Michael says, looking at his brother hard, then drops his eyes and goes back to shovelling.

Their mother is still smiling, but she doesn't look happy anymore.

Stephen turns around to see if their father saw, but he's flipping a big, floppy newspaper page, folding it in half how all fathers do.

Stephen turns back around, reaches to pick up his shovel and bucket, and there's Michael's shovel, smacking him on the back of the hand again. Their mother's brow furrows and she looks like she wants to go out and say something, but she doesn't; she just watches.

"Mine," Michael says again. "Mine." Because he's just a small boy and everything is about him. Not that this changes much with age.

Stephen looks like he wants to apologize for stealing Michael's sand, but he's just a small boy, too, so he can't articulate his feelings well enough to do that. So he just looks hurt. Then Michael smacks his brother again with his shovel, and he hasn't even done anything; he's still just sitting there, cupping his hand.

"Ow!" Stephen finally says. And then, because even though he doesn't like speaking, he feels like he has to so that

Michael will stop: "Sorry," he says, and rubs his hand.

Michael smacks him again with the shovel, this time across the face.

Their mother's trembling now, and the eleven-year-old version of Michael is right beside her, and he can tell that she wants to help, but their father's out there and he should be doing something, but he's not, he's just reading and reading and flipping and reading some more.

"Do something," Michael's older self whispers against the screen door. "Do something . . ." But he doesn't know who he's talking to—himself, his mother, or his father. Maybe everyone.

Outside, the younger Michael cracks Stephen again, right on top of the head, and now he's smiling.

Their mother's crying just a little, her hand on the handle of the door.

"That hurts!" Stephen screams, and both hands are on top of his head.

Michael drops the shovel and whacks his brother with the bucket this time, in the ear, and blood starts to run from it. The bucket is half full of sand.

When Michael stands up and pulls his arm back to hit him again, this is when the boys' father finally looks up from his paper and does something.

Watching his father from inside the house, from eight years in the future, Michael's able to see how unaffected he looks. He just seems a bit bothered that he has to break the boys up, that he's being forced by their behaviour to act like a father. He rumbles in his truck voice and makes Michael put the bucket down before he can swing it at Stephen's head again. Stephen's lying on his side, bleeding from the ear, crumpled. The boys' father tells Michael to go to his room. He tells Stephen to go inside and have his mother look at his ear. Then up goes the paper—crinkle-crinkle-fold-fold—and Michael and his brother do not exist again.

When the boys' mother left them or was abducted by aliens or whatever happened to her, Michael thinks his father just turned into another brother. Older, taller, but still just a boy, like he and Stephen. *Fathers can only be fathers,* Michael thinks, *when they have mothers around to make them what they are.*

Stephen stumbles toward the glass door, and there's the boys' mother, finally able to move, finally able to exist again, pushing the door open, fussing over Stephen, getting bandages and iodine from out of the cupboard above the sink.

The younger Michael—walking through the sliding door and into his older counterpart's body, the two now becoming one—doesn't go to his room like his father told him to. He stands in the corner of the kitchen, watching his mother and Stephen. Just staring from the corner. He watches their movements very carefully, as if trying to figure out what they're doing, what went wrong. His brother and he were just playing in the sand—just playing, having a fun time. What's the matter? Why is he in this kitchen? What just happened? The older Michael searches in his head for this memory, but it simply isn't there.

Stephen looks at his brother over their mother's shoulder while she leans down to attach the bandage to his ear. Michael's looking at him and he's thinking—and this is one of the clearest thoughts he's ever had—he's thinking: *What's wrong with me? Why would I do that to you?*

Once she's attached the bandage to Stephen's ear and given him a good, strong hug, she turns around, swivels her head, and her eyes find Michael in the corner.

She sees something in his eyes. The look she gives him says: *There's something rotten inside you. I can see it. There is something* wrong *with you. You're a terrible, terrible boy, and I don't love you anymore.*

The boys' father walks in the back door, folding and tossing his newspaper on the kitchen table. He looks at no one.

Growing up, Michael remembers sometimes wondering what it was that their father stuffed into him and his brother, what things he crammed into those holes that he dug in them both. Standing in that kitchen—the smell of his mother, the sad, confused eyes of his brother across the room, and his father walking through the wreckage as if none of it touched him—Michael realizes that those things his father dug and stuffed into his children were pieces of himself.

Pieces of himself that he didn't like.

7

WINDOW IS REPLACED by rock. Michael's nose nearly touches its smooth surface. The elevator skips past 8 and slides straight down to 7. But Michael doesn't want to see 7. He wants to see 8. Turning around, he pushes the glowing Up arrow. The wall stops about a third of the way down, but nothing else happens. He pushes it again. The elevator groans, the rock wall slides down, and the whole thing shifts upward. Michael looks above, at the row of lights, and the little circled 8 is glowing. He turns around and waits for the rock wall to slide up.

Nothing.

The wall is damp, but Michael doesn't care about damp walls; he wants to see the eighth floor. What if Marla's on it?

"Open says me," Michael says, because he's such a funny guy. "Open, please."

A thin river of water dribbles down the wall, but it doesn't open.

Below the elevator, Michael hears someone talking. It sounds like a man's voice. A voice Michael thinks he's heard before. The man is repeating something. Getting down on his hands and knees, Michael presses an ear to the floor. He concentrates very hard on the words, and soon he makes out what the man's saying: "Press the Down button. Press it, son."

A very white face bobs above a crowd in Michael's memory.

"Clown?" he whispers. "Is that you?"

The words come through a little clearer now. "Come on, son, press the button. You want to come down to 7. Nothin' on 8 worth seein' right now anyhow."

Michael stands up and presses the Down button. Another

rumble and a groan and the 7 circle lights up above his head.

The rock wall shoots up.

Then that long arm from Michael's memory comes for him again, reaches down through the darkness of this level, and he follows it up and up, to the very white face of the clown from the carnival. It's far above him, like the moon, and he's thinking a lot of the same thoughts he had when he first saw the clown in the crowd. The makeup. It looks like—

"It doesn't come off," the clown says, and grins a little.

"I know," Michael says. "You told me before. And somehow I knew it then, too."

The clown's hand is damp on Michael's shoulder, just like at the carnival.

Michael asks, "What's your name?"

The clown squeezes Michael's shoulder. His hand feels like a big sponge. Then he steps back from Michael and pulls up his pants a little.

"Don't have a name, son. Not even quite sure what one is, truth be told. But I have this makeup. And that's more than some people, you know?"

"You don't know what a name is?" Michael asks. "My name's Michael. That's what other people call me, so that's my name."

The clown just nods his head and keeps silent, like old people do when they haven't heard a word you've said but don't want to admit it.

"You don't understand, do you?" Michael says.

The clown ignores Michael and points at the hand that is holding the fourth letter—the fourth letter that Michael had forgotten he was holding until the clown pointed to it.

"What's that piece of paper?" the clown asks, as if he doesn't know, as if everyone in this building doesn't know.

"A letter," Michael says, just to be friendly, even though

he's not really in any sort of mood to be friendly to anyone.

"What letter's that, then?" the clown says.

"Can you turn on some lights in here?" Michael says, very quickly, because he doesn't want to talk about the letter, even if the clown's telling the truth about not knowing what it is. "It's dark and I want to see what's in this room."

"No, you don't," the clown says.

"Sure I do, Crimley," Michael says, and there's his name, out of Michael's mouth before he even knows it. Crimley takes no notice.

"No, really, you don't," he says. All Michael sees are his colourful moon-face and one of his damp, fishy hands floating around as he talks. It smells like a soggy dog in this room.

"Why don't I want to see what's in here, Crimley?"

"Uh," and his big, pale fish waves about in the dark, "it's just pieces of things. Little wet bits of this and that . . . you know." He shrugs. "Let's go in the elevator and read that piece of paper you have there, what do you say, son?"

Crimley's lumpy catfish hand is bugging Michael now, though, and he doesn't want to be closed in an elevator with it. It looks like it's dripping with something. Maybe water, but maybe not. Maybe a piece of whatever he's hiding in the darkened room.

"Nah," Michael says, "I'm looking for someone, and I should get going. Nice seeing you again, Crimley."

"Well, alright, son, but I'm coming with you."

"Coming with me where?" Michael asks. No one ever goes anywhere with Michael.

"Wherever you're going," Crimley answers, and hitches up his pants again.

"Well, I don't know where I'm going, really, but . . . you can" —and it's very hard for Michael to say, a boy who has no friends— "come along if you like."

The part of Michael that is a small boy, whatever part of him is still left inside, figures it'll be fun to have a clown around. Even if it's not a real one.

"But why do you want to come with me, Crimley?" Michael says, because the part of him that is *not* a boy won't let this happen so easily. "Why don't you stay here in the dark with your little bits of wet things?"

Crimley looks around, shrugs again. "There's got to be more to life than just these tiny pieces, doesn't there? Even out in the carnival, it's still just bits and pieces walking around. I want something . . . solid. Something bigger than all of this."

"Is that what Hob took from you?" Michael asks, remembering what the eyeless boy from the tenth floor said.

"Hob?" Crimley laughs. "What's a 'Hob'?"

"That tall man with the pocket watch. Top hat. Green suit. The guy who interrupted us at the carnival when I first got there."

"Oh, yes, that fella. I know him."

"Well, Hob's his name."

Crimley becomes an old man again, just staring, apparently confused.

"Anyway, did that guy take something from you? Did he put you here, in this room, with all these little wet things?"

Crimley puts a fish up to his chin, scratches there for a second. Then the other fish wraps under the elbow of the first, and he says, "Could have, yeah. Not sure, now that you mention it. I seem to recall doing something else with myself before this room and the carnival and the darkness and the wet bits. I think I was somewhere else, and I think I had bigger pieces of things, but I could be wrong." He drops his fishes to his sides. "The smell in here affects the memory, you know?"

"Sure," Michael says, but what does he know about

memory? All he knows is that his father says it's a fickle thing. Whatever *fickle* means.

"Sometimes," Crimley says, "I take the elevator down to the carnival—"

"Down to the carnival?" Michael interrupts. "The elevator leads to the carnival? To the Freekshow building?"

"Sure does. Where'd you think it went?"

"Well, I don't know."

"You think you just popped into some place *other* than the Freekshow?" Crimley laughs again. It's a funny sound—like a bunch of fat marbles rolling along bumpy concrete. "You don't gain access to anywhere you're not supposed to, son."

"But the Freekshow building is only one floor. I saw it from the outside. It's not eleven stories high."

"Yeah," Crimley snorts, "sure it's not. You're on the seventh floor of a non-existent building."

"I'm not saying I'm not on the seventh floor of a building; I'm just saying that I don't believe it's the Freekshow building. I saw the building from the outside—from both the front and back—and it's only one floor."

"Believe what you like, son, but this is it. I've only seen it from the front, though I hear there's a back entrance, too. The front and the back are on different blocks of the carnival. That's the story, anyway. And just because I can't see the upper floors from the front of the building doesn't mean they're not there. Lots of other stuff exists that I can't see. Works the opposite way, too, son: Lots of stuff I believe in that probably *don't* exist. You know?"

"I've been through the back door. There are stairs there, and it leads down into more rooms."

"You've been through the back door?" Crimley's eyes go wide, and Michael has suddenly become something important to the clown. Crimley clamps both his wriggly fishes on

Michael's shoulders, squats, and leans in close to his face. "Who let you in?"

"Some dirty little man. I don't know. He turned into a grain-sack turkey, I think, and showed me the way with his one eyeball."

Crimley licks his red, red lips. "Don't know about dirty men or turkey sacks, son, but if you say you got in the back door, then I believe you!" His sponges squeeze Michael a little too hard and Michael winces. He wonders what Hob took away from Crimley. A big piece of something, that's for sure. And Michael thinks a part of Crimley just as big wants it back.

"The elevator can't get us there, Crimley. If you take the elevator down to the streets of the carnival once in a while, then you must know it doesn't go down to the Freekshow building, right?"

"Sure, sure, son, maybe not for me. But what about for you? You don't go nowhere you're not supposed to. I just said that, didn't I? Sure I did!" Crimley stands up again, grasps Michael's hand in one of his fishes and stomps over to the elevator. "So let's see where the elevator takes you! Maybe it'll go straight into the Freekshow itself. I sometimes hear whispering from the floors above and below me about what's inside the Show. Incredible stuff you wouldn't believe!"

Crimley is too excited now. Michael doesn't want him to be disappointed when they get in the elevator and it doesn't go where he wants it to, so Michael's thinking about how to calm him down, how to tell him not to get his hopes up, that he might never find the big piece of whatever it is he's lost, that they might never get out of here at all.

But nothing comes to mind, and Crimley's happy, and Crimley thinks this is going to be some sort of big adventure. Crimley doesn't know what he's been doing in this room with all these wet bits, so maybe he's not the best travelling partner a kid could have. But they're both looking for replacement pieces, so they at least have something in common.

Maybe Crimley's right; maybe they'll find everything they're looking for. Crimley'll get his big, solid piece of whatever he lost back, and Michael won't die in a pool without his Marla.

The rock wall slides up and they get in. Michael pushes the Down button, and looks to Smithy, but the image of the turkey-sack has no words of wisdom for him.

The elevator rumbles on, and it's just Crimley and Michael against the world.

Crimley and Michael against themselves.

6

"JUST KEEP PUSHING the Down button, son. Nothing we want on any of these floors anyway," Crimley says, running his fish fingers over the lighted numbers above them.

"How do you know that? You don't know who I'm looking for."

"Well, whoever it is, they ain't on any of these floors. I've been to all these floors, boy, and they're occupied by people who've been here longer than me, so they can't be the person you're looking for—not a kid of your age, no way."

His fingers leave trails of wet goo on the numbers, blurring them.

"How do we know she's not with one of those people, Crimley? *You've* been to each of these floors, so what's to say she hasn't?"

Crimley looks down from the glowing numbers. "It's about trust. I'm trusting you that you've been in the back door of the Freekshow, so you just trust me about these six floors, okay?" And he's back to feeling the little circles again.

But what does Michael know about trust? Same as he knows about beliefs; same as he knows about memory—only what people have told him. Play to your strengths is something Michael's father always says. Your weaknesses play to themselves and don't need any help from you.

So Michael only hits the button once, to floor 6.

The rock wall slides up and reveals Crimley.

Another Crimley. An older Crimley.

"Push the button again, son," the Crimley in the elevator says. His voice is hard, edged with something. Not anger, but something just as tough. "Push it."

The older Crimley stares back at them. The room is basically the same but brighter than on 7, but Michael still can't make out the wet pieces on the floor, though some of them seem to be twitching or squirming around. Sloppy wet sounds come from different parts of the room. Older Crimley's fish hands are soggier and more limp. They're nearly dripping to the floor. He tries to smile, but it's like his clown makeup won't let him stretch his face muscles to do it. So he frowns instead, takes a step toward the elevator.

"You've come for me now?" Older Crimley says, lifting an arm to point at the Crimley in the elevator. "I should say you have, son. I should say you have." Another step and there's a squelching noise under his foot.

"Push the button," Younger Crimley says. "Please."

Older Crimley edges closer, and something in his eyes makes Michael turn around and do as Younger Crimley asks. Desperation, perhaps, or something very close to it. Desperation is something Michael does know about.

Michael punches the button.

Silence.

Shuffling.

Then: BOOM!—BOOM!—BOOM! and Michael's heart slams in his throat.

"Come for me!" Older Crimley shouts, his voice muffled like when it's cold out and you're talking through your scarf. "Come for me now!"

Younger Crimley shakes his head back and forth, eyes wide. "Not yet, old man," he says. "I'm not coming yet."

The elevator slides down to 5.

Michael punches the button.

And again. Three more times.

The little number 1 is circled above them. The wall slides up to reveal darkness. Michael can't hear Older Crimley anymore.

126

Michael looks up at Young Crimley in the elevator with him. "You get older with each floor, don't you?"

Crimley nods. Slumps in a corner of the elevator.

"And each floor gets brighter."

Another nod.

"How far down have you seen?"

"Fourth floor," Crimley says, puts his face in his hands.

"Can you see what the pieces are by then?"

"Almost," Crimley says, and Michael can barely hear his voice at all. Crimley's shoulders hitch up and down.

Michael has never seen a man cry; he uses the awkward moment to pull out and read the fourth letter:

> I was close today. Almost came back home. But now I'm faraway again. I felt him there. I was a few blocks away and I felt him. How do you stand it? How does his brother stand it? I'm sorry, I really wanted to come home.
>
> I'm lonely. Nothing is good where I go. But I can't go back to that house. I won't go back. I don't even know why I'm writing this letter. There's nothing new in it, but then there's nothing new for me anywhere.
>
> I don't think I'll write again. Writing does nothing to help anyone. We just keep circling and circling and it all stays the same, because you won't get rid of him. He's more important to you than your wife and your real son. I don't know how you live with yourself. How do you sleep at night? I hate you now. If not for abandoning your family, then certainly for carrying on with your life after you'd turned your back on us. I would have killed myself if I had to live with what you have to.
>
> You're just a selfish little boy living with other selfish little boys, and I'm glad I left. This is the last time I'll write.

Michael folds the letter back up and notices writing on the other side. Writing he didn't notice when he unfolded it just a few moments ago.

Michael folds up the letter, puts it in his pocket, unsure what to think, what to make of any of this.

Crimley's eyes have dried. There are no black and white streaks on his face where tears ran. Michael wants to see the real Crimley. He wants to see what he looks like under all that whiteface. It's not as easy to feel sympathy for someone who looks like a clown.

"Crimley, we're on the first floor. Is this where you usually get off to go to the carnival?"

Crimley nods. He's not here. He's back on the sixth floor watching himself get old. Or maybe in his mind he's on the third floor, watching his skin wither, his mind flake away, his breath come in short gasps. He's probably dead on the second floor. Rotted. Along with whatever pieces he's been keeping for company.

Michael walks over to Crimley, reaches down and grabs his dead fish hand, pulls hard on his arm so he gets the idea that Michael wants him to stand up. "Go stand and wait for me outside this door, okay, Crimley?"

Crimley's head wavers, nods, but Michael's not sure he hears him. "Crimley, I have to go see what's on those other floors, okay? The eyeless boy, or somebody anyway, told me the elevator will show me something different than what it showed you. My Marla might be there. So just wait right here for me, alright? I'll be back as soon as I can."

Crimley, finally on his feet, just stares out into the black of the first floor. He wets his red lips and says, "Right here, son. Right here." He steps out of the elevator, moves off to the right, and leans against the wall.

"Just stay right there, okay, Crimley? I'll only be a minute."

The rock wall slides down again. Michael turns and punches the Up button again and again. The number 6 lights up above him, the wall slides up, and there's no crippled Crimley stumbling toward him, no wet smell, and no glistening red bits scattered on the floor.

There is only the window.

And the shape, clearer, moving closer.

Small. Red. One of those little red Bibles. That's what Michael's holding, sitting in his bed at night at nine years old. There's a page in the front of this book that has the Canadian flag on it. The space below has room for Michael to write his name and address, which he has done with great care.

It is the single most important book in existence, and here he is just holding it. He feels like he should be doing more with it. It doesn't seem enough just to hold it and read it. It needs more attention somehow. It should get a piece of every person that holds it. An exchange of some kind only seems right when the reader is getting his soul saved for next to nothing.

Reading it each night when he goes to bed, it terrifies him. And after a couple of weeks, he's afraid to open it again. Then the page with his name and address starts coming out. He accidentally catches the edge of it with his fingernail one night while closing it, and the rip gets bigger every time he opens the book, even though he's careful as can be. And he just knows he'll go to Hell if that page falls out; that's what happens to people who do bad things to this book, it swallows them, eats their souls, makes them into terrible people so they have no choice anymore. They become horrible human beings and do awful things to themselves and everyone around them. Michael knows this because he has the Fear of God in him, and that's what the fear tells him, it says, "Watch that page, son; your eternal soul rests on it. Watch it carefully." And he does, he does watch it carefully, and he breaks into cold sweats when nine o'clock comes around because that's when the Book needs him to read it, needs to tempt him to rip out that first page, to prove that he's a worthless, selfish little boy doomed to Hell by his own actions.

Every night he opens it up, not reading a word (he can't even see the words inside anymore; they're blurred streaks, and he's too much a sinner already to deserve to lay eyes on them), waiting, waiting, nearly itching to tear the page out. Since the flag of his country is on it, too, he'll be a traitor if this page falls out—a traitor who'll get stabbed with pitchforks, jabbed with steak knives, and have his insides roasted while still alive, charred skin over an open pit of flames, and the flames will eat him up a bit at a time, and—

The page falls out into his lap.

He doesn't understand it, but he's somehow relieved that the page fell out. It fell out straight onto him, straight into his lap, and nothing happened. Nothing at all.

He picks the page up, turns it over in his hands. It's just a piece of paper. Nothing special about it at all. Michael's flesh isn't roasting, his eyes aren't being stabbed out. It's all lies.

The whole thing. Lies.

Suddenly, the scene shifts and Michael's on his bike, riding it down the street. A few blocks away from his house there's an overpass. It's pretty high up, so he can't see anything on it. He figures it's empty, because he's just a kid and doesn't understand that traffic travels up there as well as on the road down here.

There's a small chunk of concrete sitting underneath the overpass. Michael stops his bike close to it, picks it up. Nothing on that overpass, anyway, and he feels like throwing this big piece of concrete around a little. So here goes, up and away. Street noises are pretty loud down here, so he doesn't hear the concrete chunk land, but then he doesn't much care, just felt like throwing it. Its weight felt good in his hands and his shoulder aches a bit from tossing it up so high and so far.

Riding his bike home, and here comes a car behind him. Going really slow, puttering along, maybe out for a Sunday drive. Old guy. Face stern. Both hands on the wheel, like all old people drive.

Suddenly the old guy's right beside Michael, and his mouth is moving, but Michael's only hearing old words, words he doesn't understand, but he stops anyway, pulls to the curb, and the old guy pulls over in front of him. The motor of his car turns off, sputters, pops a few times, and finally settles into some quiet clicking noises.

Old car, too. A matched set.

Now this old guy says things about rocks and overpasses—that much Michael gets—but then he goes on to say stuff about dead and dying women, driving off the road because some kid, some idiot kid, he's saying, threw one of those rocks right up onto that overpass and smashed her windshield, and did Michael know the old guy was a retired cop and he's going to report Michael, has already called the police and ambulance to go to the scene, and that he'd been watching Michael from his apartment balcony on the fifteenth floor, and saw it all, watched him pick up that little chunk of concrete, throw it, and pedal away on his bike like nothing had happened, no one was dead or dying, and he's just going back to his world of men and boys, but now that's over, it's over, and the old guy's words slow down a little, begin to make sense to Michael, and suddenly it's an event like no other before it—

—Michael's crying for some lady who crashed her car because he threw a rock and it hit her windshield, a rock he didn't know could hurt the lady because he didn't know the lady existed, because nothing exists outside of men and boys, and maybe the retired cop, too, that saw Michael kill that woman.

That's what the cop says he thinks. He says he's not sure, but from what he saw, it looked pretty bad, that if she's not dead now, she's probably pretty close.

The old cop's words are plain English now, and Michael's heart speeds up, the tears blind him. He's falling off his bike onto the street. The cop tries to help Michael up, saying he'll take him home to his mother, but he doesn't know that Michael doesn't have a mother.

But his father—well, Michael thinks his father might be

mad. Not because Michael killed someone, but because he killed a woman, and women don't exist, not to his family, so he'll want to know how Michael managed that, how he managed to kill something imaginary. His father will forget about it, and by him forgetting about it, Michael will forget about it, and everyone will be happy with the fact that this woman drove off a bridge because of a big rock Michael threw through her windshield. Even the men in this dead woman's life will be happy because they will no longer have to pretend that she was real, and they can go back to being a normal family, like Michael's, and so this—all this stuff, all these thoughts—is making it easier for Michael to stand back up and get on his bike again, remember his address, tell the old copper, then set his feet on his pedals to carry him home, the cop's rumbling old car right behind him, sounding for all the world like his father's voice. That distinctive language of Father to Son.

And they're two parts of a messenger, the cop and Michael, they're two parts of a whole. One part is coming to tell a boy's father about the terrible thing he did; the other part is just coming home, just returning to where he started this morning, to put his bike in the shed around back and go play a board game with his brother, maybe build a model by himself, and try not to think about rocks and overpasses and, least of all, women.

Michael is disconnected from the scene. Entirely. He's watching it from outside his body.

His father stands in the doorway. The cop's car is still rumbling in the driveway. The cop has his hand on Michael's shoulder, standing next to him, explaining to the boy's father what happened. The cop's face shows emotion. Michael's father's face is stone. Michael's face is stone. The old cop says it was an accident, but it doesn't matter because a person

133

is dead. *Don't forget "or dying," copper,* Michael thinks. *If you're gonna tell the story, at least tell it right. You don't know she's dead. You don't know.*

And she wasn't.

After the old cop made a phone call, other cops came to the house and told Michael and his father so. The woman was cut up pretty badly, had broken several ribs, and had fractured her skull. But she lived.

So nothing happened to Michael. He was not taken away. The cops said the woman did not want to press charges. She was just happy to be alive—had said she always thought something like this was waiting for her. And that she would die when it found her. But she didn't.

She didn't.

And at the end of it all, Michael is left with his secret buried deep inside, now proven true and unbreakable—the one he's keeping to himself forever, the one he learned from The Bible, and from his father:

We answer to no one.

Back in the elevator, Michael punches the Down arrow five times fast.

He thought he could explore the other floors, but he's a coward, just like Crimley. And there goes another part of him, sucked into the window, probably on the fifth floor, maybe the fourth as he passes them. That chickenshit part of him worth less than the dirt and filth that cakes every inch of this place.

But at least he's leaving pieces behind, like breadcrumbs.

So he can find his way back.

The elevator door opens and Crimley is gone. Where Michael told him to stand and wait for him now holds only stale air. But straight ahead of the elevator, on the opposite side of this first floor, is something that wasn't there before.

An open door. The back door to the carnival. The same door Michael passed through to get to Marla and the shadow versions of the card players. Michael sees in the shaft of light coming from outside that the stairwell immediately inside the door is still there.

The thought of Marla being down there again kicks Michael in the chest. He steps quietly off the elevator, walks across the wooden floorboards, toward the light, the door, the stairs, blood pounding in his ears, at the back of his skull.

He thinks: *If she's there again, I'm not going to listen to a word she says; I'm just going to grab her by her soft hand and lead her back out through the Freekshow, take her home. Her home can become my home. We can live together, and be there for each other, and laugh together about men and how they don't exist, never did exist, and the silliness of people who think they're real, that they're anything other than big yellow claws, digging, digging, claws so big they could hold fifty screaming babies. That's what I'm going to do.*

And now Michael's halfway to the door, his feet nearly in the light, almost there. He has to skirt around the hole where the stairs start or he'll fall down them and kill himself, shatter his kneecaps, crush his skull, lose an eye, so he skirts the staircase and walks right out the door, into the sunlight.

Looks to his right.

The mime that was drawn there before has changed—not washed off, like one of those two little boys said it might be, but changed. Replaced.

It's a simple drawing of Hob, eyeless, in the same position as the mime was, neck bent, strapped to a pole, dead or waiting to die. Written on the belly isn't "poke here," but three words, brief instructions, in bold, black ink—fresh, much clearer than the outline of the body:

Michael looks back at the stairs, then glances around for the little boys from before, but they're nowhere.

He looks at the words written on Hob's belly again.

Directions. These are the two directions he's been going all his life, his eleven-year life that seems to have taken forever.

Michael's mind feels older than eleven, and his body aches like an old man's. But then what does Michael know of old men? What does he know of age? Age, like so many other things he thinks about, is just a word, just an idea with no roots or connections to him. And he's tired of not being in control.

So he decides in no uncertain terms that he's going to call down the stairs for Crimley twice, then Marla three times, and if neither of them answers, he's going to go back up that elevator and head for home. He's going to go drown in the new pool by his brother's and father's hands, and he won't even put up a fight. It's a silly decision, but he's not just going to be pulled around by the nose in hopes of finding something he's lost. As a man—as a boy, even—he has to make a choice, and he has to stick by it so he can say he did what he wanted, without having the option of blaming someone else if it turns out to be wrong.

Michael walks back into the building. "Crimley!" he shouts, leaning over the edge of the staircase, looking into the black below.

He waits for a noise. Nothing.

"Crimley!" That's two, and no answer.

If he cries about this, he's not going to do it until he gets in that elevator.

Why didn't you stay where I told you to, Crimley?

"Marla!" Michael's voice sounds flat against all this brown, all this dead wood. It sucks the noise into it. He wonders if this building's only still standing because of the shouted words of the people who live inside it.

One.

A fly lands on Michael's forearm. He takes no notice.

"Marla!"

The fly tickles, but Michael's staring down into the dark,

concentrating, listening hard. He doesn't brush it away.

Two.

He breathes in so deep, he thinks his chest is going to burst. And here comes number three, here it comes, rushing up Michael's throat, ready to burst out in all capitals—

—when he glances down at his arm and there's a fly, a fly he's suddenly going to name Joey for no other reason than it's the first name that popped into his head. He lifts his arm up to his face and exhales the waiting word slowly, ever so quietly, covering Joey's tiny body in his unused "MARLA!" Joey's wings ruffle a little, but still he stands his ground. This is the type of fella that was needed back at Michael's house when his father was taking all comers. Joey holds tight and just cleans his feet in front of his face.

And now Joey knows who Michael's looking for. Michael wonders if Joey will stay with him when he walks down the stairs; he wonders if he'll come along to protect him, like Smithy did, maybe show him where to go, what to do, where his Marla is, then give her name back to her. So she'll know who she is, and so she'll know who Michael is. So she'll know he wants to mean something to her.

Michael hopes desperately that Joey will come with him, that he won't just fly away, because he needs someone with him.

"You comin' with me, Joey? You gonna help me?" Michael whispers. Joey's washing and he's washing. He doesn't say anything, but he doesn't leave Michael's arm, either.

Michael starts walking down the steps. His heart feels like it's right inside his head now.

Beating at the sides of his skull to get out.

5, 4, AND LOWER

AS THE LIGHT fades and the staircase becomes steeper, Michael wonders how well Joey will do in the cold down here. Already it feels colder than before, Michael's breath crisp in front of him, the wooden steps sounding more like metal as he descends.

He reaches the bottom and passes through the doorway that leads into the room where Marla and the card players were last time. The table and chairs are still there, and the light above shining down onto the raw wood, but there's no one in the chairs, not even shadows. Michael gets closer and sees that the shadows *are* still there, but they're not proper shadows anymore; it's like they've been deflated. They're just puddles of black lying limp in this seat, hanging draped over that one. Moving around to the other side of the table, Michael touches one of these shadow-puddles—the one that had been Jimmy, who'd been hiding cards in his beard—and it's sticky, but firm, like chewing gum right after you take it out of your mouth. On the seat is a playing card, sticking halfway out of the puddle.

The only seat without a puddle is the one Marla had been in. That one's clean, just plain wood. Michael sits down in it and looks around the room, lifts Joey up to his face again.

"If you were Marla, Joey, where would you go, and how would you get there? There's no way out of here, except back up those stairs."

Joey looks around, turns this way and that. He jumps off Michael's arm, flies up to the green lampshade, and just sits there, flitting his wings every now and again. Michael imagines he hears Joey's feet singeing from the heat of the light.

Michael peeks up under the lampshade. Regular old light bulb. Nothing special.

Joey's really strutting now, like maybe he's upset that Michael's not picking up on his message, that it's so obvious and that Michael's such an idiot because he can't see it.

Joey lifts off, bobbles around underneath the lampshade, bouncing off the bulb a few times.

Michael remembers something he saw his father do once while changing a light bulb. Licking the tips of his fingers, Michael stands up and reaches under the lampshade, twists the bulb quickly, just enough so that it's still in the socket but also enough to make it go out.

Complete darkness, and Michael feels Joey land on his arm again, very still, as if satisfied that Michael understood him. Michael sits back down in the chair and waits. For what, he doesn't know, but maybe, he hopes, when his eyes adjust to the dark, he'll see something, maybe a way out.

A couple of minutes pass, then low along the bottom of the far wall to Michael's right is a thin, thin line of light, just like the ones along the sides of the tunnel he dropped into from the charcoal.

From the chair, Michael drops to the floor, crawls on his hands and knees to the strip of dimly glowing light. Looking along the bottom of the wall, he sees that it runs the entire length of the room, side to side, and is about an inch from the floor.

"So what do I do with it, Joey?" Michael looks at the spot on his forearm where he guesses the fly might be. He wonders how many of Joey's little eyes are watching him. "Well, don't just stare of me, Joey; look at the wall, figure it out and tell me what to do."

But Joey doesn't do a thing. It's getting even colder in here without that light on, and Michael knows flies don't like the cold. Flies are all about warmth. During cold days at Michael's house, they all hang out at the window, soaking up the sun or bouncing around inside lampshades, excited by the heat. Michael always figured the inside of a lampshade to a fly was like a sandbox or a toy store to a kid. All sorts of fun in there, all sorts of comfort.

Michael runs his finger along the line of light, blotting it out where he touches it. Nothing happens. He crawls to one corner of the room, moves slowly along the line with his finger, crossing over to the other side of the room. Maybe if he touches it all, it'll trigger something. He knows he's being too much like Stephen with his comic book ideas, but what else is there?

When he makes it to the other side of the room, runs his fingertip to the edge of the wall, still nothing happens.

"What now, Joey? Come on, put a little thought into it, will ya?"

But Michael doesn't think Joey's in a thinking sort of mood. He imagines he feels the fly shivering against his arm.

Dumb idea, anyway, Michael thinks. But what if, maybe, he just has to run his finger along the line of light again the opposite way?

Michael crawls across the floor again, this time slower, making sure he covers up every bit of light as he moves along. When he reaches the other side, his hands are nearly numb from the cold. He pulls his finger back from the corner he started in.

Nothing.

Michael stands up, defeated.

Joey drops off his arm onto the floor.

"Joey?" Michael says, and the word falls flat out of his mouth like a brick.

There's a low groaning. The thin bar of light he'd traced opens up, gets wider and wider. A giant, bright red mouth, yawning. The whole wall moves up, just scrapes straight up into the ceiling. The mouth is so bright now that Michael can't look at it.

When the noise finally stops, Michael cracks an eyelid. The room is now twice its original size, but there's no floor in the new portion that just opened up. There's a flashing neon sign, like the ones motels have, hung at the far end of the room. It says:

Then the groaning sound again and the floor begins to tilt, trying to dump him forward. Michael tries peeking over the edge of the empty space in front of him, but below is only darkness, lit up for brief red instances as the neon sign flashes. Michael hears gears in the floor creaking, an engine working. He's running out of room.

Michael backs up against the wall behind him, clinging as best he can to it. Closes his eyes tight and waits to fall forward into the blackness.

A cold wind blows up from below. It fills the room. Fills Michael's lungs. Freezes the spit on his lips. He feels a scream coming up from inside him, but has no time to let it out before he's falling through the air, down and down.

It seems like a very long time before he hits the bottom, but when his eyes pop open after landing on his back, he still sees the flashing letters above him, and they're only about twice as far away as before.

The hazy red lights up the room with those quick, buzzing flashes, and as he gets to his feet, winded from the fall, he sees where he has to go next. There's a dark little hole dug into one of the walls. It's low, right near the floor of this new room, and probably just big enough for a boy his size to fit into.

Michael hopes the hole doesn't go down deeper than this, that maybe it carries on straight sideways or angles upward, but he knows that won't be the case. Things like the Freekshow need to be buried, and the deeper the better.

In a sizzling neon flash, Michael sees a tiny, black speck next to his shoe. He squats down to get a better look. It's Joey. Curled up, feet tucked in, lying on his back, dead. Frozen, Michael guesses, as he watches his own red breath plume out in front of him.

Another single-use friend. Just like Smithy, just like the dirty little man, and maybe just like Crimley. Just bridges, designed to help him across to the next section of the path.

What if that's all Marla is? Then what? Michael thinks. Maybe she's dead or gone somewhere else, having found whomever it was she'd been waiting for. But maybe she's at the end of this little hole beside him, too.

Or maybe it's all just leading him straight to Hob.

The cold makes him tuck his arms into his T-shirt, so that now, crossing the space between himself and the wall, he's an armless little boy, squatting, getting down low to squeeze into a small hole that probably leads to somewhere even colder. Somewhere he might die, turn to an icy block of confusion.

Michael squeezes his shoulders together to fit into this hole, slides his body inside like a worm. He wiggles, squirms, and it's a little bit wider on the inside, but not much. He's in and lying flat on his belly, shuffling farther inside; no more buzzing red bursts of light, just the sound of his movements against the cold, hard-packed dirt.

Up ahead, he hears muttering, sees a tiny pin of light. Flickering, like it might be candlelight. He shuffles up some more, feels the slight decline in the surface as he moves along. Down and down, and he wishes he had Joey with him. He wishes Crimley's painted face was lighting the way ahead. He wishes Smithy were tucked under his arm. He wishes and he wishes, and he's been down this road before.

But it's okay for now because here comes some warmth, here comes that candlelight. Branching off from this first little tunnel on the left is the source of the light—a hole leading into another room. As quietly as he can, he shuffles the few remaining feet to the opening and looks inside.

A man sits on a stool, all alone in the room. A candle burns on the dirt floor, near his feet. He's holding a few sheets of crumpled paper, and Michael sees his lips moving as he reads what's written on them. Shadows of the pages flutter on the low ceiling above the man's head. The man looks like one of the people from the carnival. He lifts his eyes from his pages, sees Michael, scowls, and says, "Go on, then, I'm rehearsing," and waves his arm. "Go on!" he says again.

But it's cold in this little tunnel and Michael wants to sit by the candle for a while, if only to warm up his hands.

"May I come in, please?" Michael asks.

"No, boy, you can't," the man sneers, and waves his arm some more, impatiently.

"But I'm cold and just want to—"

"Well, you can't, so move along," the man says and looks back down to his papers.

Michael waits, shivering, his teeth chattering.

The man looks back up at Michael. "Oh, for chrissake,

boy, can't you see I'm practicing my lines? What if I'm called up and I meet him in the streets and there I am, clueless about what I'm to say or do?"

The man's long, black beard flops around as he speaks. Michael watches its shadow on the ceiling. The pages he holds and his beard combine to create a shadow-puppet show for Michael.

"Called up to meet who?" Michael asks.

The man snorts, swivels on his stool to look at Michael more directly.

"'Who,' he says. Who do you think, boy? Same 'who' you're rehearsing for, you fool. The *boy*," the bearded man says, candlelight dancing in his eyes. "The *boy*."

The way he says the word, you'd think there was only one boy ever created. You'd think that if he were selling the word, if it were his to sell, he'd be asking a million bucks, a truckload of gold.

"Have you seen a man with a painted face come this way? Or a woman?" Michael asks. Michael knows he doesn't have to describe the woman, because she's the only woman in the whole wide world.

"Clowns, ya mean?" the man barks at Michael. Flutters his pages in frustration.

"Well, he's not really a clown, see, 'cause his makeup—"

"Clowns are the next door down, boy. On the right. But they're probably rehearsing, too, and clowns aren't any fun to bother. It's not all fun and games down here, you know. We can't all just act like little kids, tunnelling around, bothering people whenever we want. This is a job, and it's not the easiest work in the world, either. So push off, kid. Go wriggle around somewhere else. I don't have time for your *enthusiasm*."

"My enthusiasm?"

"Yes, enthusiasm," the man says. "Like right then, perfect

example, when you asked *enthusiasm* like you did. You want an explanation for why I want you to go away. You need validation even for dumb stuff like this. You're weak, but you're enthusiastic about being weak. No matter what I say to you right now, you're going to question and question and question. Even right now, this very second, all that're in your head are questions, swirling around in there, and you're wondering which one to use, which one will help you get to the bottom of the reason why I don't want you to come in here and warm up by my candle. Enthusiasm, boy, you've got it and I don't want it. Not down here. So ship out and leave me alone, got it?"

And he's back to his pages, mumbling, turned fully away from Michael.

The clowns, the man says, are the next door down, on the right.

Michael shuffles farther down the tunnel, the air getting crisper as he goes.

About a minute later, Michael sees another slice of light filtering out into the tunnel, coming from the right side. He shuffles faster and almost doesn't notice the sound of paper rustling beneath him. It's down near his waist before he stops to find out what it is.

He barely feels his forearms where they connect to the cold dirt through his thin shirt. Struggling to work around the bottom of his shirt, he pops his hands out and finally gets hold of the paper underneath him. He rolls on his side as far as he can go, shirt twisted up near his neck, his back against the tunnel wall, and brings the paper up to his face to see the words. But he's in between light sources, so he hardly sees anything at all. He stuffs the paper into a pants pocket, wrestles his shirt back down, his arms stuffed back inside, and pulls himself farther through the tunnel, closer to the clown hole, and the sound of louder and louder voices.

Stopping at the hole opening, Michael's breathing heavily now and one of the clowns inside spots him immediately. He points Michael out to the other clowns in the room. They all turn their heads from their conversations and smile at him. The one that spotted Michael says, "Hey, little fella, where ya off to?"

All these clowns have nearly the same makeup on their faces, with just a few differences in the colours and designs. Mostly blacks, whites, and reds, with a few browns thrown in here and there. A lot of swirls and some hard, thick lines down their jaws. But this is normal makeup, Michael can tell even from here, not their real skin, like with Crimley.

There are candles burning all over the room. Michael feels the heat on his face, and wonders what the clowns would do if he just wiggled straight in and sat with them. He has a quick, terrible vision of them ripping him to pieces, then painting his corpse to look like one of them, so he decides to ask first.

"Do you mind," Michael begins, and the thought of them saying 'yes' sends a shiver through his entire body, "if I come inside for a minute . . . just to get warmed up. Just to even warm my hands up, please? I'll only be . . . a minute. Please."

"Sure!" says one of the clowns. "Squeeze on in here!"

A couple of them hurry over to help Michael through. When they grab onto him, their skin is so warm Michael lets out a thin moan.

"Damn, you're cold, kid!" says one of the clowns, as Michael's dragged through into the warmth.

"Been crawling," Michael says, standing up, popping his arms out of his shirt's sleeve holes, and pointing to the hole behind him. "In there. For a while." His teeth chatter. Suddenly there's a warm blanket draped over his shoulders and he closes his eyes, sucks the heat into himself. Buries his face in the fabric of the blanket and inhales.

It smells like makeup and dirt.

Michael is brought over to a spot with four or five burning candles, invited to make himself comfortable. He sits down, moves his hands over one of the flames. Another moan escapes his mouth, this one thicker.

Looking around as he defrosts, he sees mirrors propped up in different parts of the room, clowns in front of them, applying their makeup, laughing, joking, and holding sheets of paper in their free hands, occasionally glancing at them, their lips moving.

"What are you rehearsing for?" Michael asks. "The guy back a little bit up the tunnel says you're all rehearsing for something. Is it some kind of show?"

"Some kinda show, alright, chum," says one clown, a rail-thin guy whose head nearly touches the ceiling. "Only show in town," he finishes, turns to Michael from the mirror he's sitting at, grins.

"That's right," says another clown, a short, pudgy one, with pimples all over his face. "The carnival is the only show worth being in. What part are you playing?"

"Part?" Michael asks. "I'm not playing a part. I'm looking for Crimley and Marla. My name's Michael."

Everyone stops what they're doing. They look at Michael hard. Their eyes in the candlelight look like brown, shiny marbles. Michael has that flash again of them ripping him to pieces, then someone laughs, and the rest follow his lead. The moment passes.

"You're the one the Show is for! Spider wants it to come off without a hitch," says the pudgy clown.

Then Michael sees a smiling face across the room.

It's Crimley.

"Crimley!" Michael shouts. "Where did you go? Why did you leave the spot next to the elevator where I asked you to stay? I said I'd only be a minute!" Michael's on his feet, excited, moving to hug Crimley.

Crimley pushes Michael to the ground before he can get his arms around the clown's waist. When Michael falls, he knocks over a couple of candles, and the room gets darker.

"What are you talking about, son?" Crimley says, and Michael's looking at him from the floor, and he knows what Crimley looks like and this is him, this is his friend, Crimley.

"It's me," Michael says, but he knows by the look on Crimley's face that he doesn't recognize him, and he can already feel control slipping away. "Me . . . Michael, from the elevator. Remember?"

"I was never in any elevator, son. And my name ain't Crimley. Now we're putting the Show on for you, sure, like we promised Spider, but—"

"You mean Hob," Michael says. "Is that who you mean? The tall man with the green suit and top hat?"

"Yeah, Spider, like I said, son. Quit interrupting me. Where did you get this Hob crap from?"

"Well, I know him as Spider, too, but only 'cause of the way he walks—the way he looked once when he walked, I mean. His legs, you know?"

Slipping. Slipping.

"Yeah, whatever," Crimley says. He's looking at Michael like he hates him, like he'd enjoy nothing more than kicking his teeth in.

"You don't remember me?" Michael says. "Not at all?"

"Never seen you before," Crimley says, and leans in close to Michael's face, "in my *life.*"

And this *is* Crimley. Michael sees that he's not wearing makeup. The makeup *is* his skin. And because Michael's very, very foolish, and because he's a little boy—an unthinking child for just long enough for him to speak, to spit the words out and immediately wish to have them back, like he's always wishing for things he can't possibly have—he says, "You're not a real clown. That's not even makeup—it's your face."

The others in the room overhear. Tears spring to Michael's eyes. He has betrayed Crimley, his friend. It's in Crimley's eyes the second the words are out of Michael's mouth. He does know Michael. He does recognize him, but for whatever reason he wasn't supposed to have been out there on that elevator, and now Michael's ratted him out. Whatever he is, he's not a clown, and now they all know.

He is not in his place. He is not where he should be.

But Michael didn't know any of this until Crimley told him with his eyes, and now Michael can't take it back, and the clowns are moving toward Crimley, more candles getting knocked over as some of the clowns move toward him without watching where they're stepping, so it's even darker now and Crimley brings his hands up to the sides of his head; his eyes are smouldering, burning holes into Michael's skull, and Michael's sorry, he's done it again, and he can't control anything, even the things he says, the things he does, they hurt everyone and he's stupid stupid STUPID, everything he touches turns to garbage, and one of the clowns is hovering just on the edge of the circle that has formed around Crimley, one finger extended, stretched out to test what Michael said, to test the truth of it, and there it slides down—

—Crimley's face, terrified—

—and the finger comes away and the designs on his face have not changed at all.

There is the tiniest moment of silence.

And then they fall on him, teeth bared.

Rip him to pieces.

A candlelight glint from one of the mirrors across the room catches Michael's eye as he turns his head away. The number 5 is carved into the dark brown frame of the mirror, above what's inside: an object, twisting, shoulders hunched, larger than when Michael last saw it in the sixth-floor window of the Freekshow elevator.

The sound of flesh tearing suddenly seems worlds away, and Michael's eyelids droop. He falls back against the wall, watching the man in the mirror—and now he finally sees that it is, indeed, a man—growing larger and larger, his arm waving, as if in greeting. But even as Michael thinks this, the slate is being cleaned; he sees the man's hand motioning, wiping something, maybe Michael's mind, his memories—

—and suddenly it's very quiet.

Stephen's sitting in front of Michael. They're in their room. Stephen's sticks sit between them, silent. There are tears in Stephen's eyes. Words come out of Michael's mouth, but he's not saying them. He's a puppet, someone's hand in his back. And the words just keep coming.

"It's true," Michael's saying, because he knows Stephen's not the brightest kid on the planet, he's saying, "It's true—you're a ghost, you're not real. Dad never wanted you. He only loves me. To him, you're a shadow of me, just a tiny, confused piece of what I am."

Michael feels the smile on his lips, but he's not pulling the muscles to make one.

This is a different kind of cruelty. Michael's discovering that he doesn't have to raise a finger to get this feeling. *That's the thing about secrets,* Michael thinks. *Even when they're discovered, or maybe even when you know they're not really secrets at all, they're still inside you. They dig and nestle, and there's no way you're ever getting rid of them. Telling the secrets just buries them deeper, where they sprout stabbing roots, which grow and grow.*

A tear drops from one of Stephen's eyelids. His weakness

makes Michael want to strangle him, and that pushes more of these words out of his mouth.

Michael couldn't feel it then, back when it was happening, but sitting inside himself now, detached, he feels a small chunk of himself, rotting, growing mould, decaying; a black skin thickening over it, creating a solid little box that covers the secret—the secret that is no longer true, but that he can't get at anymore. He waited too long and it has grown into him, funnelled through his veins, and it's just as much a part of him as anything else.

Michael dug this hole, though; he removed the dirt, shoved it deep inside to protect himself, then shovelled the dirt back on top, packed it down hard.

It's Michael's and it's spreading inside him.

"See? Do you see now? You don't even belong here; you don't belong with us at all," Michael says to Stephen. "You're no one's son. You don't belong to anybody. And one of these days, dad is going to tell you all the same stuff I'm telling you and then he's going to make you leave. He won't care if you starve or freeze to death, either, and why should he? You're not his. You don't exist. You're just some lost ghost, following me around, wishing, hoping to be part of a family. Anyone's family."

Stephen's just crying and crying and shaking his head— no no no, say it ain't so—and no, Stephen, it ain't so, but Michael's not telling you that. No way you'll get that out of him. Because something has twisted inside of him. Gone black and cold and put down roots.

But there's something wrong with Stephen's face now, and it's not his weak little-boy tears, or his red, puffy eyes, or his quivering lip—it's something else, something blurring his features. Michael blinks hard to clear his vision, but Stephen's face keeps warping, changing shape.

He's starting to look like Michael.

Michael rubs his eyes as hard as he can; he rubs them till they hurt. But Stephen is Mr. Potato Head and everything keeps rearranging itself, and soon he'll be Michael completely.

When Michael's own face starts to change, bones shifting like icebergs beneath his skin, his stomach begins to boil, and he suddenly feels so—

—cold. In this hole.

Michael's teeth are chattering and there's nothing but blood-soaked clowns standing in a circle in front of him, staring down, picking their teeth with jagged fingernails.

Something red and skinless twitches on the floor at their feet.

The clowns move apart and go back to their stools and mirrors, wipe their faces clean, brush their hair, reapply their makeup.

Michael sits for a few more seconds, staring at the puddle of muscle, blood, and bones, then he whispers a weak apology to it, gets slowly to his feet, and moves toward the hole's exit.

No one even looks at him; he squeezes through into the cold tunnel again.

What have I done to my friend? What have I done? Michael thinks as he crawls on his belly, exactly how he should, a snake in the grass.

Up ahead, he sees another warm light flooding into the tunnel, this one bigger. He wishes it was impossibly hot, searing his flesh from his bones, turning him to ash.

Michael continues crawling down and the tunnel opens up to a height where he can nearly stand. One of those thin, glowing lines—this one thicker than the ones back near the elevator—runs along either side of the dirt now, lighting his way. Hunched over, he pulls out the piece of paper he'd found earlier, moves over to one of the lines of light, and tries to read it.

There's nothing written on the paper. Not a word. Michael flips it over.

Nothing.

He shoves it back in his pocket and moves ahead to the next opening.

🐚 Poking his head into this new room, Michael sees that it's a lot bigger than the last two: the ceilings are higher, there's a tiled floor—black and white squares—there are torches on the walls instead of just candles on the floors, and the room is full of people of all different kinds.

In one section, a group of mimes strapped to poles play at being dead, little boys practice poking their bellies and giggling. The mimes occasionally scratch an itch, and they have to start again. In another corner is a grey pig sitting on a wooden stool, posing for a man drawing the pig's face on white balloons, a pile of sticks beside him, little plastic Xs to paste over the pig's eyes when he's done drawing. There's a man standing next to the pig, holding a leash, making sure it doesn't scamper away.

Closer to the back of the room is a long stretch of dirt where men pull dead horses back and forth. A man stands to the side and directs them, commenting on facial expression or the position of their bodies, the rope they hold over their shoulders, which is wrapped around the horse's neck. Nearby is a pile of the dead horses. Extras, maybe, for when the skin starts to peel off these ones. The men are singing what sounds like a railroad song; some are smoking grey pipes and coughing out the words.

Fat men on unicycles, a few scattered clowns, a knife thrower, a man holding a giant hammer, laughing, slapping another man on the back over and again. Men stumbling around with pies on their faces. Jugglers. Leopard women. Midgets. Puppies. Dog-faced men. Magicians practising card tricks, practising slicing women in half in long black boxes.

But looking closely at one of the women's faces, Michael sees that it's wooden. Only sawdust filters to the ground as the magicians work through the box. Another man sits near the head of one wooden woman and sculpts her features with a small chisel and hammer. Different coloured paints sit on a table next to him.

And nearly everyone with sheets of paper in their hands, either mouthing lines or speaking them out loud to each other.

A filthy hobo walks toward Michael, so he pulls his head out of view, steps back a few feet into shadow. The hobo ducks out into the tunnel, whistling. Michael follows him quietly, making sure to take his steps when the hobo does so he doesn't hear the dirt crunching under Michael's feet.

The tunnel swings to the right and widens out more. Now Michael can stand up completely. But the lights running along the walls also widen, giving off more yellow glow, so Michael has to hang back a bit more to stay in the dark. When the hobo gets to the end of this new hall, Michael watches him disappear down a hole in the floor.

Michael waits a few seconds, then runs to where he last saw the hobo. There's not as much light here, because the lines of light thinned out a few feet back, so Michael almost falls right down the hole. But he catches himself, leans over to try to see what's below. He notices there's an old ladder sticking up just out of the dark round spot. He grabs the top of it and heads down.

Beneath him, Michael hears someone talking, so he waits about halfway up the ladder and holds his breath.

It's a woman's voice.

It's Marla's voice.

And it's all Michael can do to hold onto the ladder as blood rushes to his head and little white dots appear in his vision.

He still hears her talking, but she's getting farther away, her voice fading, and he can't wait any more, so he climbs down the remaining rungs of the ladder.

He finds himself in another tunnel. Completely dark. No light sources coming from anywhere.

No sign of Marla.

And suddenly he's so sick and tired of all of this, and he can't take it anymore, it's all piling up inside him, these actors, these players, this dirt, filth, confusion, darkness, he just wants to find her, his heart hammering, gasping for air, standing there, one hand on the ladder, the other holding his chest, and his mind speeds up, starts shooting thoughts through him, quick thoughts, stupid thoughts, thoughts that will get him killed, but then he wonders by whom, who will kill him, he's all there is, he's the only real thing in any of this, this show, the script these people are reading, all of it his, but it's dark and kids are afraid of the dark, and he has no clue at all where he is, and now Marla's voice is gone, and he's left alone again, he's lost her because he can't move after her, he's paralyzed and he's terrified but he's strong enough to get through this, it's not beyond him, he knows it's not because he's after something he deserves, something every boy deserves, even if that boy isn't quite who he thinks he is and—

—he needs a mother and

(here it comes)

a WOMAN in his life

(his thoughts become gunshots in his skull)

—a replacement to the one he's lost

GUNSHOTS IN HIS SKULL

Calm down, take it easy, Michael thinks. *Calm down, move your feet ahead, move them, Michael, move them, follow.*

The voice.

It's still there. Listen.

Just move your feet; put one foot in front of the other and follow it. You can hear it now, can't you? Sure you can. It was always there; you just weren't listening hard enough. Slowly now. Concentrate on the voice. On your Marla, because she's yours, Michael. She's yours, no one else's.

So he follows the voice to the end of one black hall and through the next.

Then:

Bluish light. Up ahead. And the voices clearer—both the hobo's and Marla's. Michael walks and walks, and then the voices stop and he sees the hobo turn into the blue light. Marla doesn't turn with the hobo.

Michael keeps walking and he's nearly to the opening and he's sick to his stomach because she's not here, somehow he lost her, and it's so unfair, so unbelievably unfair—

—then his foot kicks something stiff, solid. He looks down and it's Marla. Slumped against the side of the tunnel wall. She's not breathing, but it's not because she's dead, it's because she was never alive.

Wooden.

Her face painted on, glowing, leering up at Michael. He slides down beside Wooden Marla, slips his tiny hand into her hard, chiselled one. The fingers aren't that well done, kind of blocky, not at all like his Marla's.

Michael turns his head to look at her in the gentle blue haze coming from the room the hobo went into; he hears familiar voices in the room, many of them, filtering out into the tunnel. Marla's eyes stare straight ahead; the colour is a little off, but whoever painted her face got the almond shape of them right.

With Marla on one side of him, the end of his world on the other, he remembers the look of concentration on the wood artist who was painting the wood woman's face back in the black-and-white-tiled room. And he remembers that the wood artist was the only person without a script.

The only one of them all without a script.

Reaching down, Michael strains to pick up Wooden Marla, her legs straight out, stiff across his arms. She's heavy, but Michael finds the strength. Marla stares ahead as he walks— her face still glowing, even away from the blue light—leading his way.

All she needs to be now is his truth, his life.

✿ Back at the tiled room, Michael rests Marla up against the dirt wall, just outside the hole where all those performers are warming up for their big spotlight in the carnival. Farther down the way, he sees the clowns filing out of their little hole, all cleaned up and heading out to let their stars shine. They're silent; Michael imagines them picking their teeth as they walk.

Michael pokes his head into the performers' warm-up room. Everyone is still practising, but they seem more relaxed now. People are getting comfortable with their roles. Before he goes in to talk to the wood artist, Michael watches him work for a while.

The man is bald, with a thin mouth and very small eyes, close together. His back is hunched; if he stood up from his stool, Michael thinks, the hunch would stay in his back— weighted down by the unwavering stare of wooden women. He's wearing light brown slacks, covered with dirt and paint. He is fat and his chins disappear into the flesh of his chest; his brown button-up shirt is open at the top, long, grey hairs sprouting in every direction.

Michael watches the magicians put down their saws and go off to little stalls carved into the walls to get dressed: black capes and black hats and black shoes.

The wood artist is alone.

Michael tells Marla he'll be right back. He imagines she smiles at him, then he walks into the room.

"Excuse me," Michael says, quietly, when he's standing on one side of the wooden woman the man is working on. He chisels her mouth, the middle of the top lip, the indent part. He's leaned in very close. His forehead wrinkles roll like waves.

Michael tries again: "Mister?"

The man in the corner holding the pig's leash glares at Michael. The pile of sticks and Xs and balloons is almost gone. The balloon guy, the leash guy, and the pig all look so tired. Michael wonders if this is all they do, if this is their only role, their whole life down here.

"Mister, I . . ." and Michael has to remember what he's going to ask him, why he came in here. It seems so silly now, thinking about it. Standing in front of this man who creates and paints wooden women. "I was wondering if you were the one who made my Marla," Michael says. "Is she your work?"

The wood artist, who, of course, needs a name, so how about Albert—he looks like an Albert—lifts his head slowly. He's wearing the tiniest glasses in the world. The lenses look cheese-slice thin.

"My work?" he asks. His lips are chapped, weathered, and Michael wonders what he used to do before the Freekshow. Something outdoors. Maybe he sculpted giant trees into giant wooden women. "What work is that, friend?"

"I'll go out into the tunnel and show you, okay? I'll bring her in."

When Michael turns around and heads toward the exit, a big woolly bear on a unicycle nearly runs him over. Someone barks instructions at the bear. He's pedaling like mad. One of the magicians steps out of his little stall and, like Michael, nearly gets run over. The magician curses, waves his hands around, says a few words in a language Michael doesn't understand, and the bear disappears in a white puff of smoke. The unicycle pedals itself a few more feet, then falls on its side, kicking up a small cloud of dust. The magician and the bear trainer get in each other's faces and start yelling.

Out in the tunnel, Michael lifts Marla gently from the ground, swings around, and carries her through the opening.

A man in fuzzy squirrel pyjamas is walking around the room pulling torches from the walls and swallowing them, then bringing them back out of his throat still lit.

Michael sets Marla down in the dirt at his feet. "Here she is, Albert."

Albert doesn't look up.

"Mister?"

Albert lifts his eyes.

"Here she is," Michael says, and steps back a little so Albert can see her.

Albert squints, pushes his cheese-slice glasses up his nose. Sniffs. Looks up at Michael. "What's that, then, friend?"

"What do you mean, 'what is it'?"

"Well, just what I said: what is it?"

"It's a wooden woman," Michael says. "A woman made out of wood." He nods and smiles. He wants very badly for Albert to understand this.

"Women aren't made out of wood, friend. Where did you get that idea?" Albert shakes his head and sets back to work, painting the wooden woman's face in front of him.

"But you're working on one right now, Albert. I watched you carve her, and right now, this very second, I'm watching you paint her."

"Is that what you see?" Albert says, and chuckles, his flabby neck and belly wobbling about.

"Of course that's what I see," Michael says, and feels the coldness that has just slipped into his voice. Michael doesn't have the patience for these kinds of conversations anymore, not like he did with Hob. Back then it was new and different. Now it's just confusing and unhelpful, and he feels the muscles of his face stretching to look like the tired pig-leash holder in the corner. "That's exactly what you're doing. I'm watching you do it. Can't you feel your hands working on her? Can't you see that you're shaping her and painting her face?"

"My hands are working, I know that," Albert says. "But what I'm working on, I have no idea. If you say you see me creating wooden women, then I suppose that's what I'm doing."

Michael is silent for awhile as Albert returns to his work, chipping away at the bridge of the woman's nose, painting her ears and eyebrows, rubbing a cloth over it all, smoothing it out.

Then: "Albert? Can you make her real again?"

Albert looks up at Michael, startled, but there is no anger in his eyes, just confusion. "Who's that now, friend?"

Michael points weakly to Marla, sitting on the floor, her face trying to glow. But Michael's already losing hope.

Albert follows Michael's finger. "Ah, yes. Is she a friend of yours? Why do you make her sit on the ground like that? And what's your name, anyway?"

"My name's Mr. Head," Michael says, because in this sad moment, he can't remember his real name. "Hob named me that."

"That's fine, Mr. Head, just fine," says Albert, and tries to smile at Michael, but can't seem to get it right. He just winds up looking like he stepped on a tack.

"Well, I guess I should be going, Albert," Michael says, defeated, and bends to pick up Marla. Albert suddenly stops him, putting a meaty hand on his shoulder. He looks around the area of his workspace nervously, looking for something, then leans in close to Michael, like Michael's one of his wooden women, ready to sculpt and paint.

"I lost my sheets," he says, suddenly panicked. "Lost 'em." And he's starting to sweat, water sprouting from those wrinkle-waves in his forehead. "You seen 'em?"

Albert knocks over paints and chisels and sandpaper and everything else on the table next to his stool. His cheese-slice glasses slip to the end of his nose, fall to the floor. They bump against one of Marla's feet. Groaning, he tries bending to pick them up, but his belly gets in the way. Michael reaches down, grabs Albert's glasses in one hand, and is about to hand them over when he looks down at Albert and the lenses start slowly opening up, growing bigger and bigger, and oh boy, it's happening again, another memory that can't be one of his because he never did those things, those awful, terrible things, but here comes another one, and all he can do is watch the glasses expand until they swallow him, a small 4 carved into the lower right part of one of the lenses, because who needs elevators, this is all happening at once in one place, no need to move at all, and here it is, the man in the lens swirls, spins closer, just enough to blur his face, his arm no longer waving, but holding something, a matching something in his other hand, long and thin, communicating, beating out a rhythm, and Michael can't see anything at all now, except—

—dad. His father.

They're together, but this time it feels different. Not like the sandbox. This time it feels like things between them are alright. But this memory can't be Michael's, either, because things were never alright between him and his father.

They're sitting on the beat-up picnic table in their backyard at the old house. They're smiling; maybe one of them just said something funny. Michael's father is looking at Michael like he loves him properly, how a father should love his son. Michael sees his father's lips moving, but no sound comes out. The words aren't important anyway. What's important is that they're laughing and understanding each other. The words they're saying aren't barbed, aren't clouded by expectations of how the other person should react. Nothing they're saying is of much importance, so they're able to say it freely. Their guard is down, and Michael doesn't know what planet this is taking place on because it's an alien landscape to him. They have never been like this. Ever.

Michael's cramming a bologna sandwich in his mouth and listening attentively to whatever his father's saying. His father finishes talking, ending his words with a grand sweep of his brawny arm, the clatter of knives and forks as his fist comes down on the table, hard. Michael and his father explode into laughter.

Michael's crying, but it's good crying because it's tears of laughter—but still, *still* this memory isn't his. It will not attach itself to him. It just floats in front of him and says, *This is not yours; this could never be yours.*

Michael's father brings something out of his pocket now; it's shiny and round, very small. It's a ring. A wedding ring. *His* wedding ring, he's saying, and smiling dreamily.

But Michael's father is not married.

You're not married, dad, Michael thinks at him. *You have no wife. You have only sons, and they are your world and you are their world and if there ever was a woman in any of it, she's long gone, and maybe you chased her away so stop holding that ring up to me in the sunlight, dad, just quit, I don't want to see it.*

And now the sound starts filtering in and Michael's father is saying something about Michael's mom and where she went when she left, and his face is serious, but Michael doesn't want to hear this, he begs his father please, please stop, but his father's lips keep moving, and Michael has to stop this, he has to stop this, he has to—

—stop doing this.

Michael has to think clearly. Think in sentences. Full, complete sentences. Michael always panics and panics and then everything swirls out of control and nothing makes sense anymore.

It has to stop.

Michael breathes in slowly. But he refuses to bleed out this time.

The picture comes clearer, movement slows down, but the sound fades again. Michael's father's face is shining bright. Michael feels calm. His father tells him something awful, but he's smiling and Michael tries to remember this moment again. This moment when his father told him and his brother what happened to mom. Where he put her, or where she went, and why she left or didn't get a chance to leave. Michael thought he didn't want to hear it, but he has to hear it, it's all he wants now, so he's struggling to remain calm and listen hard for the words.

The skin of Michael's face feels loose, like it's about to slip entirely off his face. It's grey and slipping from his bones as his father talks.

That's when the videotape in Michael's head rewinds, goes back to the part where they're laughing and having fun, goes back to that someone-else's-life. His father's talking again, and it's the part where he gets serious and takes out his wedding ring. The volume fades in now. His father says, " . . . mother left a note."

The ring in his hand seems to be pulsing with sunlight.

"She just had to go, son," his father says. "It's not at all that she didn't love you. She loved you dearly, and she loved me, too, but we'd grown apart and this ring wasn't enough to hold us together anymore."

Whose father is this? He's lying. He's lying. But Michael feels his mouth open wide. He's swallowing it. Gobbling the lie down.

"I tried to convince her to stay, but she wouldn't listen," Michael's father says.

Tape rewinds again.

Back to the laughing, and now his father's showing Michael that note, but it's not the same note as the one Michael found. Not even the same paper. Michael's father says his mother left her family to run off with some other man, that she was tired of being tied down, tired of Life With Children.

Rewind.

Laughter. The ring. Lying and gobbling. Lying and gobbling. Choking on it.

Rewind. And rewind.

And Michael feels the skin on his face loosening more, dripping, dangling from his jawbone. He tries holding it in place, but it's slopping through his fingers—

Rewind.

Michael is face-down in his face, chewing lies, swallowing them, and listening for more. Now he doesn't even need to see the ring, or to watch his father's eyes act sorrowful and watery. All he needs now is for someone to push the Rewind button again.

To keep feeding him:

His mother was a spy; no one knows what happened to her.

His mother was killed in a storm after she left; a falling tree crushed her car.

His mother's a rock star; she went out on tour and never came home.

His mother's a lunatic; she's been locked up for her own good. Seeing her again would only make it harder on all of them.

His mother doesn't exist. Boys don't have moms. Only girls do. Not that girls exist, you understand, but if they did, only they would have moms.

His mother's an alien and her race came down in a big silver spaceship and took her home.

Rewind the tape, dad, Michael thinks. *Tell us again how mom left, where she went, and why she's never coming back.*

None of it is ever his father's fault. He knows that. The letters tell him that. Not his father's letters, though, the *real* letters. The ones Stephen and Michael found. Their mother left because of Stephen, because something's wrong with him. Michael's remembering these things now, just like he's remembering eating his face, the lies swimming in it. And it was the best-tasting thing he'd ever eaten in his life, because it's everything he wanted to hear, everything he wanted to believe.

You're a good father for making us forget. Only a good father like you would spare his children the real reason their mother left them: Stephen is not a good boy. He is not a good son. He drove his mother away. His own mother.

Then, a sudden wave of white noise hissing, becoming—

—" . . . gotta be here," Albert mumbles.

Albert, the wood artist, mumbles.

"Hey, friend," he says, then, and waves a fat paw at Michael, trying to get his attention. Michael licks his dry lips. Tastes face.

"Help me look," Albert says. "I need them sheets. They got stuff on 'em. Instructions. Things I have to do."

Michael's heart sinks. Albert's been put down here, too. He has a script; he's just lost it, that's all. And now he needs it to know what to say to Michael next.

"Ah-ha!" Albert says suddenly, produces a few crumpled sheets of paper from under a tray of grey paints. He still doesn't quite manage a smile, but he's closer now than before.

Albert bows his head and looks to be scanning the first of the pages, line by line. Michael leans over and sees that there is nothing written on it. Albert flips back and forth between the pages, and Michael clearly sees that there is not a word on any of them. Michael pulls out of his pocket the blank sheet he found in the tunnel.

"One page missing," Albert says, and he looks close to panic again. "I had another one, this isn't all of them, where'd the other one go? Right here, right here, there was another, oh jeez, I lost it, I lost the most important part, I can't believe my luck, this is unbelievable, absolutely—"

Michael unfolds the blank page he's holding and pushes it under Albert's nose.

"Here, Albert," Michael says, and when Albert's eyes see the page, he stops talking, drops the other three or four sheets and scans this one, back and forth, his lips mumbling words Michael can't see. Albert's mind and heart are desperate over ideas that do not exist.

Michael picks up Marla from the floor and heads for the exit. Before he leaves, he walks by balloon guy, reaches out and grabs two of his sticks. He'll be two balloons short now, but Michael's sure the Show will go on. Pig-leash guy just keeps glaring at Michael as he walks away.

Looking back over his shoulder, just before stepping out into the tunnel, Michael sees that the angry magician who had made the bear disappear from its unicycle is still arguing with the bear's trainer. Shouting, spitting, screaming, the magician waves his hand around again and the bear comes back in the same puff of smoke in which it disappeared. A little confused, it finds its unicycle, gets back on it, and happily pedals away.

3, 2, AND LOWER STILL

MARLA, FORGOTTEN BY her creator, seems to cling to Michael as he carries her through the tunnel.

Her face isn't glowing quite as much as before, and it's harder to see through the surrounding darkness. The rooms on this level seem empty now. Everyone off to the Show. Performing for no one but each other.

Michael's feet carry him and Marla down the ladder at the end of the tunnel again. Reaching the bottom, Michael feels his back pocket to make sure the pig-balloon sticks are still there.

Sounds from the blue-lit room at the end of the hall are louder than before. Men's voices, rumbling through the walls of the tunnel.

Michael walks toward the room, wondering what to do with Wooden Marla. As he gets near the entrance, he decides to leave her out in the tunnel where he found her. The glow of her face is nearly gone; Michael doesn't want to watch the dark of the tunnel swallow its last bit, so he moves away, enters the blue-lit room.

Inside:

Once the bright blue from the walls wears off and Michael can see people, he realizes he knows them. Michael knows them all.

The room is huge. People chat and hold glasses in their hands, filled with different-coloured liquids. A giant punch bowl sits on one round, orange table. On another table, this one much larger, an assortment of liquor bottles. Beer, wine, and other kinds Michael doesn't recognize. His father only ever drinks beer (Corona) and wine (red).

Behind the rumbling voices and occasional bursts of deep laughter, there's another sound, but Michael doesn't know where it's coming from. Then he sees a splash of yellow against all the blue, far at the back. It's the big claw, the pool digger. No one sits inside it, though, and the noise gets louder.

Finally, Michael settles his eyes on what's inside the claw, and it's those babies. Fifty screaming babies, piled on top of each other in the claw—because it's big enough, and that's all the reason that's needed. They're wailing and clutching and pulling, and it's nothing but mouths and waving arms in there. Michael wonders about the babies on the bottom. Crushed, suffocated, dead babies. Or maybe they're not dead. Maybe they can breathe because the script calls for fifty screaming babies and if they're dead, they can't scream.

Beside the big yellow claw are the Numbers. The black Numbers and the white Numbers—they're all here. Papers in one hand, drinks in the other. Laughing, joking, smiling, their tools scattered about at their feet. A couple of the Numbers tickle the topmost babies' bellies, but it does no good, they just go on wailing.

Walking toward the punch bowl is Michael's third-grade teacher. Beyond him is a group of boys from Michael's school. They're all eyeless and moving their heads back and forth in front of the papers they hold in their little hands. Michael catches bits of what they're saying and it's all bragging and threats and awkward silences—everything school is made up of.

A bunch of wooden little girls and women are stacked beside the boys, faces glowing, limbs stiff. But the boys are blind and concentrating. No one is interested. Michael thinks about bringing some of the wooden females out into the hall for Marla to talk to.

Other faces: The man from the convenience store down the street; Michael's next-door neighbour, Mr. Shipley, walking around in a rough square with his lawnmower, practicing, waving hello to no one; Spencer Crahan, the first boy to talk to Michael in kindergarten. Everyone milling. Acting. Some with props, others just with their scripts.

On one wall is an enormous portrait of Smithy, his giant, sloppy eye staring, glassy, wet. On the opposite wall is a portrait of Joey, Michael's fly friend, magnified, huge, hundreds of eyes, thin little legs. Blood on them. The portrait has caught him in mid-clean.

Everyone Michael knows or has ever known is here: The dirty little man, now standing under the portrait of Smithy. Joey, Smithy, and the dirty little man—Michael feels pieces of his dead uncle in each one of them. Leaving words for Michael to find. Directing him. Helping. Communicating.

The card players are here, too. Even Crimley. Not ripped to bits, but standing over near someone else Michael recognizes:

Hob.

Tapping his cane on the hard, blue floor.

Hob and Crimley are in deep discussion. Michael hears Hob's tapping cane like banging on a thick, wooden door in his head. His feet carry him toward them, and there's a drink and a drink—two drinks for the two actors, backstage, relaxing, just chatting. Then Hob turns his head and sees Michael coming; Crimley turns his head, too. They seem impossibly tall.

"Mr. Head!" Hob says, and Michael's standing beneath him. Not next to him, not beside him, but beneath him. Michael's neck is pushed back, his face straight up, like he's at the bottom of a tall building.

Crimley keeps quiet.

"I say, what *are* you wearing? Jeans and a T-shirt, like any common boy. Go into my wardrobe and put on your suit."

Hob brings a long arm around behind Michael's back and pushes Michael between himself and Crimley, toward a small door set into the wall on their side of the room.

Michael looks back at Hob, trying to feel anger, trying to feel something other than confusion, but the voices around him rumble and drive any sort of emotion away. Michael puts his hand on the doorknob and turns it.

It's a closet. A bar runs across it. On the left side of the bar, big green suits; on the right, small green suits. Top hats on the floor. Behind the clothes: darkness.

Michael steps inside because it's forward movement. He can't go back.

Michael shuts the door behind him, takes the letters out of his jeans pocket, removes his clothes, feels around for one of the small suits and a top hat, and puts them on. He puts the letters into the green pants of his suit. The material feels rubbery against his skin.

In here, shut away from the voices, Michael is allowed emotions. He is allowed to feel angry at everything that has happened, at everything that he has had no control over. This rubbery suit makes him think of Crimley's dead fish hand on his shoulder and that makes him think about the fact that no one is as they appear to be, that they are all just actors, that his life and his feelings have been scripted from the beginning of his memory, a memory that isn't even his, that has been plotted out by a creator who has forgotten him or at the very best doesn't care about his life, his happiness, and there's a sudden ache inside him for Marla, his Marla, wherever she really went, wherever she really is, if she was ever real at all. He suddenly wants someone to pay for this, to answer for these things.

To lay down and die.

And he stays in this closet for too long, and now there's

Hob or Crimley or one of the eyeless boys or some other shadow of nothing, knocking, knocking on the door, banging on it, making it shake, making the whole room shake, making Michael break into a sweat, the rubber suit pulling tighter to his skin, making it harder to breathe, and there's a faint whiff of something familiar, and Michael feels like he's not in the closet anymore but somewhere safe, somewhere he used to go to hide when he felt ignored or unhappy or confused or unloved or not loved properly, or when he missed his mother, the mother he never knew, and yes, this is so sad, it's pathetic, he knows, but the scared little boy would run and hide and cry and cry and cry in his—

—father's closet.

Michael's father is Hob and Hob is his father because they're all rolled into one for just this brief, brief moment in this closet, backstage at the show of his life.

The banging gets louder and now it's pounding and those fists are heavy and slippery and wet and sloppy; they're splashing outside on the door, so cover your face, or eat your face, because it's time, it's time, even with no hands under the glass of Hob's pocket watch, it's still time to open that door and ask that person, that adult, very politely, to stop pounding, so Michael turns the knob, and blue light crushes him against the blackness behind him.

He stumbles and Crimley's long arm and dripping fish hand drags Michael out of the closet and into the blue room again. Michael's father is standing there in Hob's suit, tapping his cane, pocket watch in hand, terribly late for something, of course.

"Where is she, Hob?" Michael says, because it's still Hob. This thing in his father's skin, using his father's flesh, its name is still Hob. And it's not just his father, anyway, he doesn't think. There are bits of Michael in there, bits of Stephen, maybe bits of other little men, too. Someone's been digging and replacing, digging and replacing. No screaming babies in the claw that did this digging, though—just cowardly men and the whisper of wooden women threaded deep inside.

The skin of Hob's face ripples a little, seems to loosen. "Who's that now, Mr. Head? Who are you looking for?" The British accent is uneven. Hob's tongue doesn't know how to pronounce Michael's father's words.

"Mom," Michael says. "Where's mom? What did you do with her?"

A mime walks by poking himself in the belly. "I'm dead," the mime says. "Dead, dead, dead . . ." His face is sad.

Crimley still says nothing. Just stands at the ready with his Fish of Doom.

"See those niggers over there, son?" Hob says and points to the black Numbers near the big yellow claw full of babies.

Michael nods.

"They stole your mother," Hob finishes, tips back the rest of his drink, turns on his heel, and walks over to the punch bowl.

Crimley leans in close to Michael. "How do things grow, boy, how do they grow?" he says, and he's talking very quickly, almost panicked, a different Crimley than the one who just angrily dragged Michael out of Hob's wardrobe. "Not much time, boy, how do they grow?"

Michael opens his mouth, but Crimley puts a fish digit to his black and white lips and cuts Michael off. "That's right, dig, dig, bury, boy, bury, you gotta put 'em in the ground, that's how they grow, that's how they die, sure, but that's also how they grow, now, come on, come on, the dirty little man told me, you know him, he's right, he's a one-eyed turkey and he's a fly, but we gotta help each other out, boy, you named him, you know him, now come on, boy, digdigdigdigdigdigdigdig—"

And Hob's back with a fresh drink. Crimley straightens up, sweating. Crimley nods at the dirty little man standing under Smithy's portrait. The man nods back, then disappears into the crowd on that side of the room.

"Filling Mr. Head's head with silly ideas, are we?" Hob says to Crimley. Crimley just shivers.

"Go stand in the hall," Hob says. "Stand there with your mouth *shut,* and wait for me. Do you understand?"

Crimley hunches his shoulders in like a defeated little boy, turns around, and walks slowly toward the exit.

"The Numbers didn't do anything to mom," Michael says. "They couldn't have. I didn't even know about them till they started building the new pool."

Michael's defiant, but his words feel like overcooked spaghetti coming out of his mouth.

Hob looks back to him, purses his lips, and pats the glass of his pocket watch. "Truth is, Mr. Head," he says, and keeps patting, pat-pat-pat, "you don't know what you're talking about. You're groping around in the dark, looking for questions to match your answers."

"Oh, yeah? So tell me what the questions are. Go on, tell me."

Hob stops patting his watch, drops the fake accent. The skin of his face loosens some more, starts to sag.

"You see this watch?" he says. "You wonder why there are no hands in it. And you're foolish for wondering, because you assume the watch tells time. It tells something, to be sure, but not time. Time means less than nothing down here—not that you know where you are, of course, not *really*—but even so. Time is used to measure events as they unfold. But when nothing happens—as it does at the Freekshow and at the carnival—then what do you measure that in?"

Michael waits, confused, head spinning.

"Precisely, Mr. Head. You don't. You can't. But you can *pretend* to, and that's what it's all about. Pretending. Keeping up appearances. It's what people do in the real world all day, every day."

Hob pauses, looks to be deciding whether or not to continue.

Then: "Perhaps I've been giving you too many hints and you're going to learn nothing from any of this, but nonetheless . . . Pull those letters out of your pocket. I'll show you what I mean."

Michael reaches into his pants pocket and—

(*digdigdigdigdigdigdigdig* is what Crimley said)

—pulls out the letters, all four of them. They're crumpled, but pressed flat.

Hob watches Michael sort them out, unfold them, smooth them out. But Michael notices as he's putting them in order that there's ink on only the first letter, the one he found at his uncle's place. The rest are blank. Michael frowns, scans them all, page by page, feeling just like Albert the wood artist who'd lost his script, panicked. "But where—?"

"What's wrong, Mr. Head?" Hob says, grinning, tapping his watch, tapping his cane, tapping his foot. Waiting.

"The letters . . ." Michael says. "They're just blank sheets. All but the first one."

Crimley leans in the doorway, motions with his hands for Michael to dig, dig, then pops his head back out of sight.

The mime smiles as he walks by again, little boys poking his belly now, doing it for him, his own hands free. He has taught them well.

"Blank sheets, you say!" Hob acts surprised, steps back, takes another sip from his drink. "Impossible!"

He puts his watch away and yanks the sheets from Michael's hands. Michael tries to grab them back, but Hob turns to the side and keeps Michael back with his elbow, his drink splashing on the blue tiles.

Hob makes a show of going through each sheet of paper, his mouth a big O.

"My, my, *my*, you're quite right, Mr. Head! Quite right, indeed! They're all blank sheets of paper, except this first one." He reads it aloud:

> I'm not coming home tonight. The boy makes me uneasy. You love him. I can't. You'll have to make dinner yourself. There is leftover shrimp in the fridge. Rice is next to the cupboard with the pots and pans. He doesn't feel like mine. I'm sorry. I'm not coming home tonight. I love you.

When he's done reading, Hob doesn't look like Michael's father at all anymore. He doesn't look like Hob, either. He just looks ugly. Alien. The flesh of his face just a loose bag of skin hanging from his skull. But his voice is softer than ever. Light, delicate.

"Mr. Head," Hob says. "Your poor brother drove your mother away. There was something decidedly *off* about him. But like me with my watch, you pretend. You pretend, dear boy. Just like we all do. To get by, to make our pathetic, dreary lives bearable."

Michael looks at the letters in Hob's hands, his long, thin fingers clutching them, and now his fingers stretch, heading toward the ground over top of his cane. He is working his magic. He is showing Michael what he thinks he needs to see to be frightened of him.

"So!" he says. "Let's have a look, shall we?" Hob flips

to what should have been the second letter. "Your father is a racist, indifferent man who lies and lies and lies to you." He pulls the pen from his top pocket and writes:

"Next," he says, tossing the letter at Michael. It flutters to his feet. "Letter number three, my boy!"

Hob taps his chin in time with his foot, and seems to be thinking. Behind him, in the corner where the eyeless boys sit rehearsing, the dirty little man has shown up again. He's talking to the little boys, motioning to them.

Digging motions.

"Stephen, your brother," Hob says, and puts the pen to the third sheet of paper. "Trapped in his own little world of comic books and wooden sticks. Maybe plotting with your father to drown you. Maybe teaching him the Secret Language of the Sticks. A stupid, sullen little boy, perhaps a bit touched in the head, if you catch my meaning. Certainly an idiot by most standards. Maybe all of these things, maybe none of them. But always assume the worst of people, Mr. Head. Always assume that they're out to cheat you, because more times than not, they are. So what would this letter say; what insights would it hold?"

Hob's pen moves across the page, angry. Bold lines, sharp letters:

> Spider-Man raped and murdered my mother.
> Spun her up in his web and ate her corpse.

"Your brother's lies are as fun as your father's, Mr. Head." Hob flashes his teeth at Michael and flicks the letter away from his hand. The skin of his face drips over his eyes, mouth, hangs from the end of his nose.

If it falls off, Michael wonders, *will there be lies inside it for me to eat?*

The little boys in the corner pick up their wooden girls and women, some trying to balance two at a time. Surely the women are hollowed out, though; Michael is bigger than most of these boys and he had trouble carrying just one wooden woman.

The dirty little man looks over his shoulder from time to time, nervous, maybe hoping not to get caught doing whatever it is he's doing. He points to the entrance of the room, then disappears once again into a laughing crowd. The little boys walk toward Crimley, who has again poked his head into the room. He's motioning to the boys.

"The fourth and final letter," yells Hob, and his whole body shakes now. A thin, red streak forms at his hairline, curves down his sideburns, his jawbone. His shaking skull loosens the skin enough that it comes free, flops onto the floor at his feet. No lies inside, though, just flies.

"Dear uncle, perhaps," the glistening, round chunk of bone and muscle says. "Useless, dead uncle, eaten by your father's flies. The Man Who Knew Too Much. What would he say?"

One of the eyeless boys trips; his women come crashing down around him. The other boys—the ones carrying only one wooden girl or woman—help him back up, help him re-stack his two females and carry on.

"Uncle was helpful, but frightened," Hob says. "Not a good combination, Mr. Head. Frightened of things he'd agreed to a long while ago, but that he'd since rethought. But when you're scared, you become useless. You just sit and watch as things unfold, until one day you get the nerve to try to change things. Perhaps then, if what you've done is something you think was 'good,' then maybe you die happy, and you think it's all worth it. But death is death, Mr. Head. You can be happy or you can be sad when it comes, but it still comes, and it doesn't matter one way or the other because—"

Sticks. In Michael's head. Clattering.

But it's not Stephen, because Stephen's not here. Hob's voice fades. Michael looks down at the glass in his hand. The ice cubes move around in the liquid as Hob shakes with fury. But no, that's not quite right. Something is moving *inside* the ice cubes. Spinning. Round and round. And Michael knew it was coming, the number 2 scratched into one of the smaller cubes, already melting, but not now, Michael doesn't want to see the final floor, not yet, because Hob's telling him about his uncle, and his uncle's very important to Michael, but the glass is closer, the man inside the ice cubes spinning, as always, but slower now, his face clear, the sticks in his hands moving quickly, and that's where Michael wants to look, the sticks tapping on the man's knees, against each other, inside his mind, but Michael doesn't understand because he doesn't understand that stick language, never could, but the stick sounds get louder, thicker, chunkier, and soon . . . slowly . . . words form.

Bits and pieces of syllables tie themselves together, cling to one another until Michael recognizes their movement, hears their motions as they would sound sliding across his tongue, his teeth. Words that mean something. Words that come from the man spinning in the ice cubes. The man whose face Michael knows. Whose love he knows (though not as it should be). Who is not a man, cannot be a man. But there he is, melting into the water as he teaches Michael his language.

Stephen. Michael's brother. Middle-aged. Their father's age.

And Michael wants to ask him: *What are you doing in there, Stephen? Why are you teaching me your secret language? Why are you so old? What happened to you? What happened to us?*

And it's over, this is the end of the line. Michael thinks he's a mime, that he's dead, that he should be teaching young boys to poke his belly. But Stephen's still talking, spinning and talking and even in death there's forward momentum, productive movement to get to the next thought.

This is what the words are saying, what Stephen is telling Michael, clattering out for him on his knees, against the window he's sitting at, on anything at all within reach that will make noise, create more words to make Michael understand, make him see that it's a—

Bright day. Really bright. In memory's eye, it's blinding.

Michael and Stephen are on the porch again. Weed killer

time. There it is, the big plastic bottle of the stuff. But Michael's in the wrong chair. He's sitting in Stephen's chair, to the left of the bottle. He's holding Stephen's sticks. But here comes Michael around the corner. He's watching himself from his brother's chair.

Somewhere sticks are clattering, communicating, and Michael's moving his own sticks in his lap, trying to talk back. His sticks are telling him something different. The words form in his head as he learns them, translates them:

IN WHOSE MEMORY'S EYE IS IT BLINDING?

What do you mean, whose? Michael thinks. *Mine. Michael's. My memory.*

But the sticks keep clicking against each other, against unseen window frames.

NO, the sticks say. LISTEN TO ME. LISTEN TO WHAT I'M TELLING YOU.

Michael watches himself sit down in the other chair, wondering why he's not in his own body, wondering what sort of trick this is. The Freekshow and the carnival and Hob and probably Crimley, too, all inside him, making him see things, digging holes, pushing, cramming themselves in, changing his memories, altering who he is, twisting the real him into whatever they want him to be. Just like his father does. Just like everyone else in his life does.

But the sticks.

The sticks.

Pounding in Michael's ears, louder, the words coming clearer as the scene plays out: This *other* Michael lying to him about the weed killer, hey, it's cold water, really good cold water, even though he *knows* it's weed killer, knows it's poison and that Michael could die from it, but maybe he doesn't care, maybe that's what this non-Michael wants, because something is wrong with him, the reason their mother left them, all that terrible stuff he did to Michael, to other people, the things the spinning man showed him, those rotten things, and the sticks beating now, BEATING against the inside of Michael's skull, beating him down till there's nowhere to go, nothing to do but listen to what they're saying.

The words come clear when Michael watches the non-Michael put the hose to his mouth, watches his little hands spray in the poison. One thundering beat after another, driving it in, ripping him out of that other body, shredding the memories that stick to the inside of that other boy's skull, chipping it off like half-dried paint. Stuck in tiny corners, but coming off with each explosion of sticks. Each clatter as they knock together, forming a barrier of truth.

And when the body Michael's in watches the other body stand up, a terrified look on its face, watches that body walk around the corner into the blinding bright day, to die or be saved, Michael doesn't care which—

Something fat and heavy falls into place. A weight that should not be Michael's. But it is.

It is.

THIS IS YOUR BODY. That's what the sticks say. They say it again and again. THIS IS YOUR BODY.

I am Stephen, Michael thinks—is *forced* to think. *I am my brother, Stephen.*

But the sticks won't let him get away with just that. They demand the full truth. They will not shield him from his real memories any more.

I am not my brother, *Stephen. I am simply Stephen. My brother is—*

And another section of his mind slaps against the inside of his skull. This is crude. This isn't the way things should happen. If he just keeps thinking, just keeps talking, keeps his thoughts moving, forward momentum, thinks about cows or

182

elevators or eyeless boys or wooden women or just anything at all that will make the sticks stop, make them stop the noise in his head, the lies, the lies, the—

—*Michael.*

My·brother is Michael.

I am Stephen.

GOOD, the sticks say. THAT'S GOOD.

And for one brief moment that seems to stretch on and on, he's not on the porch in his chair, but on a stool, and he sees himself reflected in a window, holding two sticks, still tapping out the message

I am Stephen I am Stephen I am Stephen

on the windowsill. But his hands are slowing. His old hands, his middle-aged hands. His eyes are bright, staring back at himself in the reflection of the attic window at which he sits, crow's feet near his temples, wrinkles around his mouth. His breath coming harder to his lungs than before.

And he knows the source of his broken wisdom.

Looking past the window, he's staring at himself, through time, through memory. This window, this attic window. Kept clean. Always kept clean to make sure his message could get through.

The moment stretches again, flips him back into the chair of his backyard with the bottle of weed killer, then just as quickly, to the ice cubes, the glass in Hob's hand, the bright blue room. Panning back, farther out until he has a normal viewpoint.

His proper memories—Stephen's memories—slip into place, and he's back listening to Hob's melting head rant about his dead uncle, how the flies got him and it's what he deserved because he should have just kept the secret to himself, but he didn't, he told, and flies go into mouths that stay open too long, but it doesn't ring true anymore, and he's just staring at

Hob, watching his teeth and tongue chomp out the words.

Stephen looks down at his hands and sees that he's holding those pig-balloon sticks. They're marked up now, like he's been using them, knocking them against things. Maybe his legs, maybe each other. Probably both. Knocking out a message. A reply to someone he'd completely forgotten about.

He drops the sticks and starts undressing, Hob's voice now sounding thin and wasted to his ears. He removes the top hat, drops it to the ground; then the suit comes off. He puts it all in a neat pile at Hob's feet.

Face-flies hover around Hob's head, swimming in the steaming gristle of his skull.

From the pile of crumpled paper on the ground, Stephen bends and picks up only the first letter, only the one true letter from his vanished mother. He doesn't need to put it in any pockets, and he doesn't need to pretend anymore. He wants to carry it with him in his hand, feel it against his flesh.

Naked, he walks toward the doorway of the blue room. Behind him, he hears Hob's voice, his true voice. The rumble of a truck. The same rumble Stephen's heard all his life. But he is not his father; he does not have the same size feet as him; he does not hate the same people as him; he will not tell himself the same lies as he did; and he is not the killer his father surely is.

Stephen does not turn around to look at him.

Stephen walks straight out the doorway, into the dark tunnel, searching for Marla, searching for his mother.

Searching for Michael.

DIGGING BOYS

OUT HERE IN the dark. Little boys, digging. Digging because it's what they do best. What has been done to them. What they will do to others.

As far down the tunnel as the blue light will allow Stephen to see, boys dig holes. All in a nice, neat, orderly fashion. Digging with their soft hands in this soft dirt. Beside their holes are their wooden girls and women. Sitting against the tunnel walls, glowing and waiting.

Stephen looks to the right and sees Crimley watching the boys. His eyes shine in the light coming from the room. Crimley reaches toward Stephen with a damp, spongy fish and pulls him out of the doorway, pokes his head around the corner, turns back to Stephen, whispers, "Stiff, boy, he's stiff. Faceless, too. Just standing there. Frozen. Cardboard."

Crimley pops his head into the room again, brings it out. "For all the world. Just standing there with no face attached to his head. Not that he needs one, I suppose, but still . . . I mean, *no face*. What did you do to him?"

But Stephen did nothing to Hob—nothing except walk away from him.

He supposes that's all it took.

"Nothing, Crimley. I did nothing to him," he says quietly.

Crimley nods, this different Crimley, this strangely hyper version of the sad clown he used to be.

"You were dead," Stephen says to him.

Crimley's face is turned away again, back to watching the boys dig, occasionally making shovelling motions when one of them looks up in a daze, as if confused about what he's doing, digging a hole for a silly piece of wood. Crimley is there to remind the boys of their purpose.

He swivels his head back toward Stephen. "Not dead," he says. "Not in the belly, anyway. That's where it counts. In the belly. Still got life in there." Crimley pokes himself in the stomach a couple of times and goes back to watching the boys.

"Back in the room with the clowns, Crimley," Stephen says. "You remember the room with the clowns?"

Crimley nods his head slightly, but doesn't turn to look at Stephen this time. "Clowns," he mumbles, and motions to the boys to dig, dig.

"Why did you act like you'd never seen me before? What were you trying to hide?"

"Never *have* seen you before," Crimley says. "Don't know who you are. Just met." He turns and looks at Stephen as if surprised to see him standing there, like he hasn't been standing there the whole time. Crimley stuffs his clammy fish in Stephen's hand and pumps up and down.

"Pleased," Crimley says. "Ever so." He grins, turns away from Stephen, mumbles, "Digdigdigdigdigdigdigdig . . . Come on now, children . . ."

"Where's that dirty little man?" Stephen asks, his skin starting to get cold, tight. It's a comfortable feeling.

"Said no worries. Said he's done. Said he's gone away, all through, left the Show for good." Crimley snorts at that, makes a show of slapping his knee, turns, looks down at Stephen. "No one leaves the Show. The Show, why, it doesn't need you or me or anyone else to keep it running. Take the fella in the green suit and top hat in there. Take him. He's done. He was The Man Behind The Show, son, but now he's done. Just look at him. No more to offer, I guess. Figured it was time to turn to stone, to cardboard, to ice, to whatever felt comfortable to him when he wasn't working the angles, setting someone up for a fall, doing whatever Creators of the Show do. But see, that's the thing, they're not really behind anything. They're a part of the Show just as much as the actors, just as much as any of us. They pull our strings, sure they do, but someone else is pulling theirs, you know? Not that it matters 'cause someone's pulling that other someone's strings, and so on down the line. It's all just so . . ."

Crimley trails off, puts a hand up to his black-and-white face, runs a fish finger along memorized lines in the design; an awareness of exactly what he's trying to say seems to cross his face.

"Well, you'd think someone would be at the end of that line, wouldn't you, son? You'd think someone would be responsible for this." The finger drops from his face. "But there ain't. The Show, same as every other world, just wakes up dead and starts walking around."

A few of the boys have finished digging, and now stand, filthy, waiting for something else to do.

"You gonna pop your girl into the dirt?" Crimley asks Stephen. "Better do it now, if you're gonna. They need time to grow, to change properly or something. That's what the other fella said, anyway. The dirty little man."

"How do you know him, Crimley?" Stephen says, trying like mad to grasp onto any familiar thread in all of this. Trying to make sense of it where sense doesn't seem to be. "Why are you helping him?"

"Am I helping him? Just doing what he asked is all. If what he asked me to do is helping him, then alright, I guess I am. Don't know what it is I'm helping him do, though. Don't much care, either. Now pop her in the dirt, if you want, and we'll get on with it."

"You really don't remember me, do you. You don't

remember the elevator? None of it?"

"Oh, I know about elevators, and I know about Creators and Shows and all sorts of other things that go on down here, but I can't connect any of that stuff to the people I meet. It's separate stuff. You're a fool if you connect events with people. Dangerous. Makes you lose sight of . . ." Crimley frowns. "Well, of other stuff you might think is important. Or . . ."

Crimley turns his back to Stephen; Stephen hears paper rustling as Crimley digs into his pocket. Stephen watches the back of Crimley's head move back and forth a few times. Reading lines. Lines written in reader-specific ink, perhaps by the unknown Creator of All Creators. Which, according to Crimley, is no one at all.

Crimley turns back, his face brighter, given purpose again. But he is a bad actor. His memory fails him and he can't keep his character consistent.

"Important things," Crimley starts again. "Like the elevator you mentioned. Like that. And also like finding the people you love. Because you do love people, Michael. Don't you?"

Crimley's script is old, outdated. He doesn't know who Stephen really is. He doesn't remember the old man he has become on the lower floors along the Freekshow elevator's route. But Stephen loves him for this. He loves that Crimley carries on with no attachment to anything whatsoever. An emotional nomad, just going through the motions for no good reason at all. Except to get things done, to be part of a working machine.

Most of the boys have now finished digging their holes and are standing, staring at Crimley.

"Yes, Crimley," Stephen says. "I love some people very much. But only some people. You can't love everyone. And even those you can, you have to be sure to love them properly—how they expect to be loved."

Crimley turns back to the waiting boys. "Put 'em inside now, boys. Drop 'em right in there."

Some of the boys move to their women, pick them up, and drop them in the holes they've dug. No hesitation. Others watch the first bunch, then copy them.

"Cover 'em over, kids. Shovel all that dirt back in." Crimley motions with his hands again, demonstrating, script back in his pocket.

Then: "Room for one more by the wall," he says to Stephen. "Have to dig hard and fast to catch up, but you can make it if you start now."

More digging. Always about digging. But the dirty little man has never betrayed Stephen, and Crimley's supposedly acting on his instructions, so sure: dig a hole, plant a woman, and see what grows out of the dirt.

Stephen walks over to where he left Marla sitting up against the tunnel wall, puts his mother's letter in his jeans pocket again, then picks Marla up in his arms and carries her toward the end of the tunnel. Stephen leans her against the wall. He turns around and digs, claws away at the dirt. The soil gets softer and blacker the deeper he goes, but he finds no worms or other insects. He has encountered nothing truly alive down here, and that seems right to him.

When his hole is about half dug, Stephen looks behind him to see how far along the others stragglers are. Nearly everyone has a female planted firmly in the ground—a row of shadowy blue humps in the dark—and is now standing, waiting for them to somehow sprout.

Except one other boy: the boy directly behind Stephen. It's the boy Stephen met on the tenth floor, the one who gave him the fourth letter. He's sweating like mad, chunks of dirt flying to both sides of him, hands a blur.

"It's you," Stephen says. The boy lifts his face, continues

digging. Except for the lack of eyes, he looks exactly like Stephen. The Stephen he now knows himself to be.

"No, it's you," the eyeless boy says, grins, and goes back to digging.

There is nothing Stephen can say to that.

Stephen glances at the boy's wooden woman; it's mother from the attic. The one on the couch, with her white bubble-hand touching the painting's frame.

"Where did you find her?" Stephen asks the boy.

"She's my mother," the boy says. "Who's that?" He points a grubby finger at Marla.

But Stephen doesn't really know who she is.

"Someone I need," Stephen says. It's weak, he knows, and he hangs his head and continues digging, turning his back on the boy. "Her name's Marla."

The boy says nothing. He gets to his feet, done digging, and places his mother into her hole, starts pawing the dirt back in, covering her. The dirt gradually extinguishes the light of her glowing face; Stephen looks away just before the final handful blocks out the last of the light.

Stephen finishes his own hole, moves to the wall to get Marla. He lifts her gently, walks back to the hole, places her inside.

All these boys watching, waiting for Stephen to finish. Crimley's eyes on him, too, motioning for him to cover her up. Stephen wants to claw at Crimley's eyes with his dirty nails, rip the skin from his face. This is Marla. He's burying his Marla. They're all burying their mothers, grandmothers, aunts, sisters. Boys, not shedding a tear, hoping to bring these women back from wherever they went. So Stephen can't cry. He just has to shovel the dirt back over top of Marla, then wait to see what happens, like everyone else.

Looking into the eyes of these boys, Stephen knows that if

he cries they'll rip him to pieces. They have the same look as the clowns did before they tore into Crimley. And maybe Stephen won't die; if they don't get at his belly, maybe everything will be fine. But he can't bear the thought. They're doing this together and he can't let them down.

Stephen gets on his knees, starts moving the pile of dirt into the hole where his Marla lies. She's on her side; if her legs were bent at the knees instead of sticking straight out, she'd be in a fetal position. Dead baby Marla.

Stephen feeds himself letters, lies, denials of truth. He's doing it right now. Standing behind himself, digging a hole for a lie of his mother. But creators have to take responsibility for their creations, so he's trying to just let it all play itself out. He has reminded himself who he is, but no one has told this other version of him, this eyeless version who thinks his dead mother is in his attic.

Stephen looks down the line of boys, from eyeless face to eyeless face, wondering how they each lost their women.

"Water!" Crimley suddenly shouts. "That's what's needed now, my little diggers. Nothing grows without water." He rubs his bloated hands against one another, head down, and starts pacing.

The boys turn slowly and walk up the tunnel. The eyeless boy starts away as well, but Stephen grabs his twig-thin arm and turns the boy back toward him. "Where are you going? How do you know where the water is?" And he feels so foolish, asking himself a question he must already know the answer to.

"Eighth floor," the boy says.

Stephen relaxes his grip on the boy as he remembers the dribble of water that ran down the elevator's rock wall when he'd come to the eighth floor before. But he remembers, too, how he dropped to the Freekshow's entrance to the lower levels.

There is no way back.

"But how?" Stephen asks. "We can't go back the same way."

"We didn't all come the same way in the first place. What makes you think we have to go back the same way? There are plenty of ways to get here. You took one, I took another; those other boys all found their own ways in here, too. You think this is all about you. You think all of this is yours, but it's not. You have to share."

Crimley claps his hands. "Let's go, let's go, you two!" He is a cheerleader, but he does not care whether his team wins or loses. "The other boys will beat you and they'll see their women sprout before you do. It might be important that this not happen, so I suggest you get moving."

These empty words stir the eyeless boy and, before Stephen can reach out again to stop him, he's gone with the other boys, already fading to deep blue, then black, up the tunnel.

Crimley walks by the blue room's opening in his pacing, ushering the boys away, and then Stephen sees Hob's face-flies silhouetted against the wall as they come swarming out into the tunnel. They buzz around Crimley's head angrily, swarming him, flying up his nose, in his ears, in his mouth, probably still covered in the gristle from Hob's skinless skull.

Crimley doesn't scream, but he thuds against the tunnel walls a few times, side to side. He stumbles over someone's wooden-woman grave and falls to his knees.

Stephen backs up into a corner, out of the way.

Crimley waves his arms around dramatically. Mouth wide open. Inside, small black shapes dance. Soon, there is only a faint sound of buzzing, muffled, and Crimley tips backward. He hits the wall at an odd angle and his neck twists, snaps.

He lies still.

The flies walk out of his nose, eyes, ears, mouth. They don't fly out, they walk.

Calmly. Controlled.

Stephen moves toward Crimley, his long legs curled under the top half of his body. He looks uncomfortable. The flies walk around on his face. A carpet of black, their wings shining with a hint of pale blue from the room across the way. They're cleaning. Walking back and forth, wiping Crimley's makeup off. Picking the skin clean off his face. Carriers of diseases, just stopping briefly to get another load.

As one creature, the flies suddenly lift off Crimley's head, and he's clean. No ink on his face at all. He is no one Stephen recognizes.

Stephen looks closer. He is not even a *he*.

Crimley's face glows in the dark. Radiates something that the men and boys of the Freekshow will never have. Life in the Belly. The ability to create something without destroying its identity in the process.

But whoever she used to be, she is that person again. Perhaps someone's sister or mother. Or maybe she was many people, all rolled into one and painted for the occasion.

The carpet of flies hovers over Crimley's body as if waiting for something. Stephen thinks for a moment, then he knows what to do. He reaches down and pokes her in the belly.

She does not move.

She does not say, "I'm not dead. Go away."

She does nothing at all but lie there with her broken neck. A real woman in a land of wooden fakes.

And Stephen starts to believe.

Marla sits in the cold ground behind him. Stephen needs water. There is water on the eighth floor. He has to get to the eighth floor. There are many ways to get there. Many ways for each person who needs to grow something. The flies are Stephen's way. The flies have always been his way.

Perhaps it runs in his family.

He opens his mouth wide to let them in.

⚜ Tunnel walls sweep by Stephen in tiny fragments.

He has seeing-eye flies. They help him through the dark. He has not become a fly, but flies are his escorts. Buzzing inside his skull. Rooting around in his skin. Their diseases feel warm. Millions of diseases. Thriving inside his body.

The flies do not talk to each other. They do not communicate at all, but they fly Stephen back the way he came without any trouble. Tiny travellers, alien explorers. Their spaceship is Stephen's head. Sometimes they bounce off a wall, or take a corner too quickly and catch an edge, but the buzzing covers up any noise that might disrupt their concentration.

They fly Stephen faster and faster, past the other boys in the tunnels, past the eyeless version of himself, up through the room that tipped him down to the Freekshow's lower levels. Up the stairs, where warm and cold air meet. Toward the elevator. Looking for light bulbs. Anything with heat.

And here comes the glowing Up arrow of the elevator. The flies dribble now, out of Stephen's mouth, down his chin. Stephen's skinny little finger pokes the glowing button and he hears the gears grind somewhere up above.

From the direction of the stairs on the other side of the room, the other boys call to Stephen from where they all stand trapped. Help them, they say. They have no way up. They need the water to grow their women, but they can't get up to where Stephen is. They want his flies. They swear they'll give them right back once they get up there.

Such liars.

So even though Stephen doesn't need them anymore, and even though he still controls them and *could* give them to these other boys, he sends his flies away. Out the door, out into the streets of the carnival.

All except two. He asks two to stay. They settle in his right hand for a moment while he whispers instructions to one of them. He asks it to go help the eyeless boy. They have a connection, and Stephen would feel bad if he abandoned him. Stephen has a feeling that the woman the boy is trying to grow is horrible. A terrible, awful woman. The kind that would abandon her children. But a brother is a brother is a brother.

Stephen knows the fly will listen to him, just like other flies listened to his father. He tells it to go help the boy who looks like him. But don't help him too fast. Stephen needs to get the water before he does. Stephen needs to stay one step ahead of the eyeless him. He knows this place better than Stephen.

He doesn't name this fly before it takes off because it's not his to name.

The fly shoots straight up into the air, bobbles around in the air for a moment, then zips off to the descending staircase across the room.

The elevator arrives, pings softly.

Stephen steps inside, wraps his hand gently around the second fly, and pushes the glowing 8.

The numbers light up one by one above Stephen's head. Cracks in the elevator walls split the rock; tiny drops of water seep in. The closer the lit-up numbers get to the blacked-out 8, the tighter his stomach gets.

Pings 4, 5, 6: A trickle forms in one of the cracks.

Ping 7: A steady stream runs down the wall.

Ping 8: A puddle forms at Stephen's feet as the elevator door slides up. His stomach ripples around in his guts. His chest is a fireball. He feels it working its way up his throat.

Far below him, he hears the eyeless him punching the Up arrow on the wall. The puddle of water pushes closer to his feet.

Stephen steps out. The wall slides down behind him. Its gears grind again as it works itself up for another descent.

Stephen wonders if the walls will hold long enough for the eyeless him to make it all the way up here.

It's very dark, and Stephen smells chlorine. In the blackness, he makes out tiny ripples of faint green light close to his feet; the quiet slap of water wriggles into his ear and he knows what he's looking at.

A pool.

The smell of chlorine is strong; it makes Stephen's head swim. The elevator pings behind him. He hears a faint swishing beneath his feet. The water level in the pool rises, overflowing, curling around and rushing between his feet.

And here's the eyeless Stephen, walking out of the elevator. His mouth opens and closes for a moment. A tiny black fly pops out, then the boy is sloshing through the water, leaning down by the side of the pool, thrusting his hands in and scooping out a double-handful. He stands up, doesn't even look at Stephen once, and gets into the elevator again. He's off to grow a woman. His mother. Nothing else matters. No other purpose exists for him.

The eyeless me is going to win, after all, Stephen thinks. *He is focussed, determined, and he's going to grow that awful woman into something even worse. He's going to feed her, water her, keep her in a nice place by the window so she gets her sunlight.*

He's going to take care of her.

The water is still rising. It's soaking into Stephen's shoes.

There's a faint buzzing near his head. It's not the fly in his right hand, because he hasn't opened that hand since he closed it on the first floor; it's the fly he sent down to help the eyeless boy. He opens his left hand and the fly lands in his palm.

The eyeless him is already in the elevator before Stephen suddenly realizes how to beat him.

Stephen's lips make quiet words. Words for flies' ears

only. Then the fly is up and out of his left hand again, headed toward the elevator. On its way, it dips low, gets caught in the overflowing water from the pool, swizzles around on its back for a second, then pulls itself out, squeezes under the elevator door just before it slams down.

As the elevator's gears grind again, the water level slowly rises, now reaching Stephen's ankles. He stands there in the green, wet dark, hoping the dirt he buried Marla in is soft enough.

DEEP END

THE POOL IS deep; there is no shallow end. These are wise words. Words to live by.

Looking into it, Stephen sees something moving on the bottom. White. Spinning very slowly. Water ballet. What looks like an arm raised above a head. Distorted. It could be any arm raised over any head on any creature. But it's not. It's Stephen's arm, raised over his head. He's naked.

Middle-aged and naked.

Stephen walks around the side of the pool. Its edge comes close to the rock walls of the room; it takes up nearly the entire floor. The water is up to his calves. He has no idea where it's coming from, how it's becoming more than what it was when he first got here.

As he moves around the pool, watching his older self rotate below—a blooming white blob spinning in the belly of a writhing dark green alien body—he thinks:

Water. Glass. Mirrors. Windows.

Reflections of himself. All through this journey.

Water rises, getting closer to Stephen's knees. He thinks: *The elevator door won't open if there's too much water. The elevator itself might crack apart, fall, and shatter to pieces at the bottom before it even gets up here again.*

The older version of Stephen stops spinning in the pool, looks directly at the younger version. Stephen closes his eyes, because he doesn't want to see whatever it is his older self has to show him. He doesn't want to know what else he's done, what other terrible acts he's committed, more ways he's shut himself in, turned himself off from the world.

Stephen tries hard, tries to run his mind, speed it up, get the words going, flowing, streaming through his head, shooting through his brain, keep it going, like a freight train, keep it moving, string the words together, but . . . too choppy, no speed, nowhere to go, nowhere to go, nowhere . . .

And he can't do it. He runs out of steam. His eyes crack open. Green swims in. Then white, then grey. Now his older self's eyes. No need for sticks here. So close—

So very close to falling into the pool as his feet slosh forward to the edge. Standing on the lip.

He's being pulled in, sucked in, yanked against his will toward the thing in the pool. His gut screams at him to back up, back up quickly, slog through the water toward the elevator, to GET AWAY, because whoever he thought was at the bottom of this pool is not at all who it really is. It's someone else, maybe Hob come back for revenge. So Stephen's not going near him, whoever it is. But his feet won't listen. He feels them gearing up—like the elevator, grinding away—to take the next step, to plunge him into the pool, sink like a stone.

The fly bounces around inside Stephen's right hand. He opens it up, lets the fly loose, teeters on the edge of the pool. The fly buzzes around his head, lands on the inner part of his right ear. It takes a few steps, settles inside, cleans its feet, starts to tell Stephen a story, show him what it sees.

Before Stephen topples forward and falls into the water, his seeing-eye fly tells him what the left-hand fly sees, how the mission is going, wraps it up into a quick-flash Fly-o-Vision package:

—*The mounds of dirt, heaped one after the other, lining the tunnel, except the one second from the end. This one is empty. Something dark and stiff lumbers along one tunnel wall; it looks confused, unsure which direction to go. Another shape lies twisted against the opposite wall, its legs folded under it, neck bent: the man who was not a man. But its face* still shines. Something else, smaller, perhaps a little boy, is slumped in the corner, unmoving.

—Then flying straight at the last mound, right on top of it, digging inside, tunnelling, cold dirt against soft, thin wings. Pushing through. Every moving part in motion. Dirt suddenly turns to wood. Searching for a face, a mouth. Somewhere to plant a seed, to spread the disease, to water it, help it grow. But not enough water.

—Quickly, zipping out of the tiny hole and over to the small, slumped shape of what must be Stephen's eyeless twin, unmoving; crawling about on first one hand, then the other, soaking the moisture up, then straight back through the hole in the dirt and in through the mouth, just wet enough, hopefully enough water to make her grow, bring her back, your Marla, your—

But then the Fly-o-Vision is cut off, the feed lost as water fills every hole in Stephen's head. Soaks his clothes. Washes over him, around him, into him as he drops like he's got a lead weight in his chest. Straight to the bottom.

Straight to the white blob, watching him. Waiting for him.

Two bloated arms reach out toward him, hands like fat starfish. Stephen releases the breath in his lungs, and waits.

And waits.

And waits.

Then pulls water into his lungs.

The older man on the bottom of the pool draws Stephen close, brings Stephen's ear to his face. When he speaks, no bubbles come from his mouth. No bubbles—just the words Stephen has been waiting for. Ever since this began. Ever since he can remember.

The words he's been waiting for all his life.

"Look," the older Stephen says. "Look what you have done."

❧ The sun sits low on the horizon, but the water is still pretty warm—Stephen's treading it. Tiny, tiny bubbles surface as he paddles his legs. His arms do the same, but slower. Pushing out, pushing in.

Staying afloat.

His father reads a newspaper on the pool deck. Michael smiles and cups his hands a few feet away from Stephen, squirting water as high as he can into the air. The sun is hot on Stephen's face. It has been a few minutes now and his father has not looked up from his newspaper once. His father's eyes—dull, flat, grey, washed out by the reflection of the sun—scan the newspaper. His lips move with the words.

Stephen turns to look at Michael again. He watches his brother turn to look at their father. Their father doesn't look back, flips a giant double-page spread, snaps the paper tight, keeps reading. Michael keeps smiling; Stephen feels anger burn in his belly.

Stephen knows what day this is. He knows what happens here. So he just treads water and waits to save his brother's life.

Michael's squirting the water higher and higher, treading water himself. He sinks to the bottom and bobs up again, filling his cheeks so he can blow water out like a whale when he surfaces.

Just then, Stephen's big moment arrives—Michael's head disappears beneath the surface of the water. *So swoop down and save him*, Stephen tells himself. *Get on with it. What are you waiting for?*

But Stephen's stuck. Frozen. His heartbeat doesn't even speed up. His arms pull in, push out, still just treading water. He looks at his father, who sees that Michael is under the water. His father looks at Stephen, his expression indifferent.

Stephen turns back to Michael, just watches the air in his

brother's lungs turn into bubbles as it slips out of his mouth. Between the frantic splashing, Stephen catches glimpses of Michael's too-wide eyes now and then.

Their father closes his newspaper, stands up, and walks into the house. Stephen sees him on the phone, calling the police. He watches his father talk to the cops: *Someone is dead,* his father's lips say. *My son. In the pool. He drowned in the pool. We couldn't save him.*

But Michael's not dead yet. He's still fighting. They could still save him. It looks like something is coiled around his feet. He can't kick his legs. Maybe a skipping rope, a length of string. Something that should not be killing Stephen's brother.

The boys' father hangs up the phone, finished reporting his son's death to the police.

Stephen bursts into tears. Scared, little-boy tears. But he keeps treading. Stephen's showing Michael how easy it is: *Check it out, doofus. Just paddle your legs around. It's easy. What are you doing? Just do like me. Pull in with your arms, push out.*

But Michael's not listening. Michael has stopped moving. There are no more bubbles. He sinks. Drifts to the floor of the deep end. Bumps his head gently when he reaches it. The rest of his pale body settles on the bottom.

Stephen looks toward the house. His father watches from the kitchen window. He is just a cardboard cut-out now. A faceless, eyeless cardboard stand-in. Blood dribbles from around the edges of his face where it's fallen off.

He is Everyman's father now. GenericDad. A father for the masses. A blind, groping, mad fool of a human being.

Stephen waits a few minutes, feels water sloshing around him, watches bubbles surface and pop, listens to birds chirping in the trees; then he dives under and grabs both of Michael's arms, pulls him to the surface. Using one arm, Stephen drags him to the ladder of the pool, hoists him up. He is heavier than Stephen imagined death would make him. Death should be light, easy to manage.

Stephen lays Mikey flat on the grass, looks over his shoulder to see if maybe someone is coming to help, but there's no one. Just the boys' faceless father, Stephen, and his dead brother.

The Father, the Son, and the Holy Ghost.

Michael's eyes are wide open, staring up at the sky. Stephen does not close them for him. Stephen thinks his brother deserves to see what he's leaving behind, what Stephen has stolen from him.

Stephen hears sirens getting closer, turning the corner at the end of the block. He folds Michael's arms across his skinny chest, kisses his cold cheek lightly. But Stephen's done with the tears. His eyes are as dry as Michael's.

Car doors slam; booted feet slap the driveway. People dressed in white, carrying equipment, come around the side of the house. Before they get to the body, Stephen leans in close to Michael's ear and whispers, "I'm sorry, brother. I'm sorry. You did not know it was going to be like this."

Michael just stares up at the darkening sky, getting colder.

Icy water and a faint green light.

Stephen's eyes try to pop open as something tugs on his arm. Hard. But the lids are too heavy. They feel glued shut. Stephen's lungs burn, full of water. This impossibly cold water.

He finally wrenches his eyes open as he's pulled away from the bottom of the pool on the eighth floor. The grip on his wrist is tight, unyielding.

The spinning white blob, the middle-aged version of him, is gone. As he's pulled away, it seems like the pool is twice the depth it was when he fell in.

When Stephen's head breaks the surface, the water is so high he nearly bashes it on the ceiling of the room. He splutters and coughs. His rescuer holds him as far out of the water as possible, thumps his back. He splutters some more, then feels his gorge rise as he vomits.

His legs automatically tread water—weakly; he's barely able to stay afloat. Without his rescuer to hold onto him, he would sink quickly.

When he starts breathing oxygen again instead of water, his eyes slip open. Out of focus. He blinks. Then a face snaps into focus.

Marla.

His Marla.

She opens her small mouth to speak and the James Bond of flies wings out. Bops its head repeatedly on the ceiling, searching for escape.

Mission accomplished.

"The elevator," Marla says, and there's her voice. Stephen looks at her, and there's Marla's beautiful, simple face. He gropes around blindly in the water, searching for her hand, and there it is. Marla's hand. And Stephen's crying again, like a little boy.

But it's now that he realizes that he's not a little boy. Not anymore. He's holding much more of Marla's hand than he was ever able to before. He lifts his other hand out of the water and it's older. Wrinkled. Not just from the water, but from age.

Marla smiles at him. "The elevator," she says again, and pulls on his new hand.

Far, far below, on the bottom of the pool, Stephen makes out the pale, still form of a little boy. It looks to be made out of plaster. Cracked and falling apart with the motion of the water.

When Stephen and Marla make it to the elevator, Marla holds up a finger—*one second*—then disappears under the water. Stephen has to tilt his head back to keep the water below his mouth and nose. Marla reappears, tells Stephen to take a very deep breath, then she pulls him under. The elevator wall is about halfway up when it stops, stuck. The gears grind for the last time, choke, creak, and are silent.

They pull themselves inside and to the top of the elevator. All the little floor lights wink on and off. There is nowhere to go for air. Stephen wants to swim back out, go to the air pocket in the main room, but Marla senses this and holds his wrist tight. Stephen's too tired to fight her.

Marla thumps upward hard with her fist on a discoloured square of rock in the elevator's ceiling. Bubbles pop out of her mouth, the last of her air.

Four thumps. Five.

Stephen lets some air blip out of his mouth. Two bubbles. Then two more.

Marla suddenly flips herself around in the water until she's upside down, and kicks hard once, twice, and the square finally cracks and breaks. Another hard kick and the water starts rising through the hole, up the elevator shaft.

She pulls on Stephen's arm, hefts him up through the hole until he gets a slippery grip on both sides of the elevator's roof. He hoists himself up while she pushes from below.

And now Marla is going to die. This thought is very clear in Stephen's head. It rings around inside his waterlogged skull as he gains his feet. The water in the shaft already covers Stephen's shoes.

Marla is going to die and there is nothing he can do. He does not learn. There is something wrong with him. Something very, very wrong with him. His head does not work the way it should. This will be the third death on his hands. He has the overwhelming urge, then, to just sit down and let the water fill the shaft, up over his head. Stephen wants to breathe in as much water as possible. He will breathe in, breathe out, until there is no wall, no Marla, no emotions, no dead brothers, nothing to make him think. All he wants to see is dark green water and a ladder he will never climb.

Stephen watches Marla's delicate little fingers groping around at the edges of the square hatchway. His first instinct is to step on them, crush them, jump across to the other wall, to the rusty ladder waiting to take him to freedom. Save himself.

Die or survive alone.

But he watches with surprise as his middle-aged hand reaches down and wraps its strong fingers around Marla's tiny hands. He pulls hard, leaning on the wall behind him for leverage. Her head breaks the surface and she coughs up a thick gout of water. Stephen yanks her out the rest of the way by her torso and pushes her toward the ladder.

She's breathing heavily, wrapping her fingers around one rung, then another. "Three floors," she pants. "Just three. Come on."

Stephen sloshes over to the ladder, the water nearly to his knees now. He grabs on, follows Marla up the rungs.

"Nine," she says. Stephen remembers the things he saw in the window on this floor. He shivers. He does not look over his shoulder toward the window.

"Ten," Marla says. These memories, too, make Stephen's skin crawl. They were not his; they did not belong to him. Either he stole them, had them dug into his brain by someone else, or made them up himself. Either way, he wants desperately to be at the eleventh floor. The boy he met on the tenth floor now slumps against a wall, unmoving in a tunnel in the bowels of this place. His mother, a confused abortion, perhaps stumbling through cold, dark tunnels, groping the walls for signs of heat. Signs of comfort.

Stephen follows his life up a rusty ladder, a life he didn't know he had, a life he doesn't deserve.

He's waiting to hear the announcement of the final floor, but he looks up and Marla has disappeared. Stephen stops climbing. Then her head pops out over the ledge of the final floor. "Eleven," she says, and pulls her head back out of sight.

Stephen climbs the last few rungs, exhausted; the muscles in his limbs burn. His head clears the eleventh-floor ledge. Marla is already walking toward the end of the hallway.

"Where did you come down?" Marla asks. Her words just barely make it to Stephen's ears over the sound of water gurgling up the shaft behind him; his own breath is raspy and louder in his ears than any sound coming from below. It's difficult to bring air into his lungs, and he can't answer Marla.

She looks back at him. He's suddenly very dizzy. He teeters about, trying to grip the wall, but it's useless. Everything swims in and out of focus; he's about to fall off the ladder.

Marla's footsteps sound in the hallway, then she's yanking Stephen hard out of the shaft. His feet find purchase on the rough stone floor, and he stumbles along in her wake.

"Where?" she says. Her voice is sharp, not at all like his Marla's.

"Few more feet," Stephen's able to spit out as he trips over his own feet, cracks his knee against hard black rock. The thin little lights along either side of the hallway flicker like the elevator buttons had done. Soon they'll go out completely and it will be pitch dark. There'll be no way for Stephen to identify where he fell through. The charcoal sprinklings will be impossible to see.

"Stay on," Stephen mutters. "Please."

To Marla, up ahead, Stephen says, "Little bit farther, I think." Behind him, the water gurgles closer to the ledge. If the lights don't wink out, the water will wash the charcoal away.

"The distance looks right from about there," Stephen shouts ahead to Marla. "Look for sprinklings." His lungs labour to bring him life. "Charcoal sprinklings."

Marla stoops and runs her hand around on the floor beneath her. Stephen lopes on a little more, then feels water slipping past his bare feet. Cold, cold water.

"Found it!" Marla shouts, then doubles over in a coughing fit. Stephen hears dribbles of water splashing against the rock.

The lights go out.

Stephen stumbles and falls. Hauls himself back up. Keeps moving.

In the blackness, Stephen keeps his arms straight out in front of him, sweeping back and forth until—

Marla.

"Arms straight up," she says. "I'll push you through." She bends and laces her fingers together, makes a stirrup for Stephen to push off from. He puts his arms above his head, lifts a wobbly leg up, puts a foot into her hands, and pushes down as she lifts.

His head breaks the surface.

Grey. Everywhere.

And Marla's bench.

The loose charcoal to either side of the hole slips under Stephen's hands as he strains to push himself up. His arms are jelly and there's no way he can do this. He can't push anymore. But if he doesn't, there's no one to pull Marla up the hole.

She will die.

Suddenly, from below, Stephen hears Marla scream with effort. He wills his limbs to make her effort worth it. Shivering, shaking, dripping wet, his arms spasm to either side of him, almost buckle as he grits his teeth against the pain, and finally he flops on the ground beside the bench.

He sits up, leans forward onto his knees, dips his arms down through the sifting charcoal, swings them around, groping for Marla's hands.

He touches nothing.

Marla's soft voice drifts up to Stephen, as if she's calling to him across a long, long field on a windy day: "It was you," she says. "You that I was waiting for all this time."

Stephen swings his arms in desperate circles, bellowing her name into the hole, pleading with her to jump up and grab his hands, telling her that he's strong enough to pull her up. But nearly a minute passes and still he touches nothing.

Now, from across that long, windy field, Stephen hears water slopping about. A moment later, the tips of his fingers are wet. A few more moments go by, and his hands become submerged in ice water, then his wrists, and soon his arms.

Stephen's facedown on the ground, arms frozen, mind empty. His hands bump against something below. Something cold. He grasps it gently, walks over it with his fingers as it drifts by.

Marla's face.

Stone.

Wood.

Dead flesh.

Stephen feels the curve of her neck, the shape of her lips, the bridge of her nose, her smooth forehead, feels his fingers brush against a lock of her hair, hoping for a tangle, a knot, something to hold onto.

Then she's gone.

Stephen is a murderer.

He is useless.

He is empty.

Stephen is completely naked, exposed for all to see. But there is no one here to witness his shame.

He is alone.

Everything he thought he was, he is not. Everything he wanted to be—everything he could have been—is his dead brother.

He has killed and killed and killed again. Now he will lay here and simply wait to rot.

Stephen pulls his hands out of the icy water, rolls over onto his side, and collapses into sleep.

BENCH

"IT'S YOU."

The words drift to Stephen from a very long distance. The voice seems to be coming from another planet. Filtering down through the solar system, through clouds, wind, rain. The two words mix and mingle until they become one word. Repeating and repeating. Until Stephen wakes up. Claws himself back to consciousness. Shivering, frozen, lightly battered in charcoal.

When he opens his eyes—blink, focus, blink again—Marla smiles down at him from her bench. Dry as a bone. Wearing her candy-striped glasses, her sundress.

Stephen inhales deeply, fills his head with the smell of candy canes.

And now, here it comes, her lips opening to speak—there's her voice, his Marla's voice: "It's you."

And she's really here, right in front of him. Alive. Breathing. He watches her chest rise and fall, mesmerized.

Stephen picks himself up off the ground, unashamed of his nakedness. He brushes the charcoal off his body as best he can, then sits down beside his Marla. He reaches out and holds one of her hands in both of his.

Soft. The same soft he remembers from when he was a kid.

For a moment, he squeezes so hard, he thinks he's going to break every bone in her hand. She laughs a little at this, then says his name. Just that, nothing else. Just his real name.

"Stephen," she says, and she says it with love, with the tone of someone who has missed him, the tone of someone who has missed him for such a long, long time, and has finally got him back. "Where have you been?" she says. "I've been waiting here for—" She looks puzzled, frowns, turns her head to look out into the great grey landscape of nothingness around them. "—for as long as I can remember."

"I've been waiting for you, too, Marla," Stephen says. Although he knows this woman's real name isn't Marla. But that's how he knows her now, and that's how she has come to know herself.

Marla nods, still looking a little confused. Her frown deepens; she glances at Stephen, then quickly away, as if suddenly embarrassed. "The man with the green suit and top hat . . . his pocket watch . . . where did—"

"He's gone, Marla. Don't worry about him anymore, okay? You don't owe him a thing. Not a thing," Stephen says.

And there's her smile again. That smile Stephen hasn't seen since the day she left him and his little brother.

His mother's smile.

Stephen stands up, pulls Marla gently to her feet, returns her smile, and starts walking.

They say nothing while they walk. Once in a while Stephen squeezes Marla's hand and she squeezes back.

This is all Stephen ever wanted; this is everything he does not deserve.

Up ahead is a window, floating, attached to nothing. As Stephen and Marla approach it, a strong wind picks up. Stephen sees that he's inside the window, sitting on a stool, a dust cloth in his hand. He's waving to himself. A beacon swirling out of the grey now being whipped around them. Stephen looks over his shoulder and sees a blackness creeping closer and closer, faster than they're walking. A shadow erasing the charcoal, erasing memory, erasing everything.

A great and terrible god's head, huge, hanging in the sky behind them. Stephen feels his own head balloon, stitched Xs form over his eyes.

But he's not going back; he's never going back.

"Come on," Stephen leans over and yells to Marla. "A storm is coming."

They quicken their pace, their free arms shielding their faces, hands tight to each other's. Through the rising winds, standing slightly behind Stephen at the window ahead, he sees his Marla, too, smiling her smile—copies of themselves, perhaps from some other place, some other time, waiting for them.

A great grey sheet of charcoal swipes them sideways just as they approach the window. It stings Stephen's naked skin. He grips Marla's hand tighter, struggles to lock eyes with himself in the window. His eyes connect, and he has just enough time to turn around quickly to see the shadows erase the last of the charcoal behind them; the place where they were just standing becomes a silent, black emptiness.

Then Stephen's on the other side of the window, the other side of his life, looking out onto his backyard, his heart still racing. No longer naked. Suddenly dressed in clothes he has no memory of buying, in a size he has no memory of being.

The pool he is to die in—*was* to die in—is covered over with dead leaves.

He sits on a stool, in this attic, cleaning this window with a dust rag, his hands making the habitual side-to-side movements as if of their own accord, ensuring the window is spotless so he can always see out.

Glancing down, he sees his sticks on the window's ledge.

Beside him, on a small, round, wooden table, is a stack of his comic books. Next to a *Spider-Man* comic is the original letter from his mother. The one telling her family that she's leaving.

Two newspaper clippings are set out beside his mother's letter. One has a picture of his uncle in it, the words below the picture giving the details of his murder; the other says what happened to his uncle's killer—there is a picture of his father in this one.

He feels Marla behind him. His Marla. Feels the warmth of her smile, sees her reflection in the glass.

He closes his eyes and inhales her scent.

Candy canes.

EPILOGUE

GUILT HAS MADE Stephen his brother's keeper.

Sometimes at night, Stephen thinks he hears his dead brother searching around the attic for their mother. It doesn't happen for long, and it's never very loud, but he's sure it's there, and he knows it's Michael. His brother roots around in the corners, maybe looking for more letters, stuck in some memory loop—a loop of a memory that is not his, of events that only happened in Stephen's head.

Stephen sometimes hears his brother downstairs in the kitchen, slamming cupboards. He hears him tromping up and down the second-floor hall. He presses his ear to the floor on those nights and tries to make out his brother's mutterings. He hears Michael whispering awful things to him through the walls.

Some nights, Stephen feels his brother's face near his, looking down, his burning, hateful eyes on him, just standing there, staring. Maybe he's willing Stephen to die in his sleep. And some nights Stephen wishes he would.

But those are the nights without his Marla.

Stephen only ever goes out of the attic to eat. He is afraid of what's in the house. Not always of Michael, but of what sort of world is out there, too, waiting to trap him should he stay too long. He's terrified of not being able to get back up here, back to Marla.

He has no idea what really happened to his mother. She may well still be alive.

When Marla's there, his candy-cane Marla, they talk about the sorts of things mothers and sons talk about. She knows everything about Stephen—things he hasn't even told her. Or, at least, things he has no recollection of telling her.

Maybe she's someone else's mother. Someone who lost her son, and was always sorry for giving him up, or watching him die, or whatever may have happened. And they found one another because of these events that set each other off, these series of happenings that create the world, whatever world needs creating. Whatever world people need to give them an idea of happiness, an idea of what it's like to be loved. Loved properly by people who matter to them.

And Marla matters to Stephen.

Because thoughts are powerful. Thoughts and ideas change people, change the world.

On quiet nights, when Stephen's brother isn't around, when Stephen and Marla aren't in the mood for talking, when he's not thinking about flies, or frogs, or clowns, or carnivals, or face-eating, or pools, or dead mothers in attics, or wooden women, or any of it—on those nights, Stephen thinks about him and Michael as kids. As young boys, when events weren't yet connected. When there were no patterns to follow.

When there was nothing but freezing rain and the stars in the sky.

They're in the back seat of the car—their father quiet up in front, just listening to the radio. It's dark, and raining like hell outside.

Freezing rain.

Michael and Stephen are in the back seat. They're playing a game Michael thought up one night. They play it whenever they're out in the car and whenever it's cold and rainy enough for them to play.

The game is simple: they roll down their windows a little, stick their hands out into the beating, cold rain, and see which one of them can keep it out there the longest.

The first few minutes are fine; it feels great—the wind

216

whips their little hands around; they form their fingers and thumbs into airplanes, dive-bombers, birds, anything that can fly. They giggle and taunt each other.

Then it starts to get a little uncomfortable as their fingers stiffen up and numbness creeps in. They feel the cold in their bones. The laughter subsides, comes in little fits, like they're still trying to be cool, even though they both know this is the last mile, the final leg of the journey. From here on in, it's clenched fists and stone faces.

Only one of them walks away.

They're staring each other down. No more taunting. No more words at all. Just the grim determination of small boys who will *not* get beaten by their brother at anything.

Eventually, the rain feels like sewing needles digging into their hands and one of them relents, pulls his hand inside the car, panting. They stuff their hands between their legs, rub them together as best they can, soon feeling the stinging pain as their hands finally start to warm up. The only difference is the look of satisfaction on one boy's face, while the other boy just curses mildly under his breath and promises sound defeat in the next battle.

Once their hands are relatively warm again, they sit up straight and tilt their heads backward under the back window as far as their necks will stretch.

They gaze up at the stars as they pass by in slow motion. They really have to watch closely to see them move at all. This is the best part of the car ride. Every time.

They're not wondering if there are aliens out there, or if a comet is hurtling toward earth to cause mass destruction. No creatures, no sci-fi stories. They're not even staring in awe. They are not attaching any sort of emotion to the stars whatsoever.

They are simply watching them. Watching them go by. Not looking for anything.

That feeling, right then and there, with his hand tingling, life and warmth seeping back in as the stars move by overhead, his brother right next to him, so close . . .

That's what Stephen misses most. More than anything.

But it is a memory. And it will fade, like all his other memories, and all his memories of memories, too.

Erased by events, by time, by shadows.

And I'm sorry, brother, Stephen thinks. *I'm sorry. I did not know it was going to be like this.*

Acknowledgements

—my childhood for producing the basis of several incidents featured in this novel

—my wife, Sandra Kasturi, for continuing to be the best of all possible monkeys

—The Toronto Arts Council for awarding me a level two grant, enabling me to finish this book

—Homeros Gilani for the wonderful interior illustrations

—Lee Shedden and Ruth Linka of Brindle & Glass for taking a chance on such a weird novel

—my agent Carolyn Swayze for taking a chance on such a weird author

BRETT ALEXANDER SAVORY is the Bram Stoker Award-winning Editor-in-Chief of *ChiZine: Treatments of Light and Shade in Words*, is a Senior Editor at Scholastic Canada, has had nearly fifty short stories published, written two novels, and writes for *Rue Morgue Magazine*. In 2006, Necro Publications released his horror-comedy novel *The Distance Travelled*. In the works are three more novels, as well as a dark comic book series with artist Homeros Gilani. When he's not writing, reading, or editing, he plays drums for the hard rock band Diablo Red, whose third album, *Lower the Troll*, was released in mid-2007. Savory lives in Toronto with his wife, writer Sandra Kasturi. He can be reached through his website brettsavory.com.